KU-322-384

MYSTERIOUS SOLIDARITIES

THE FRENCH LIST

MYSTERIOUS SOLIDARITIES

Pascal Quignard

TRANSLATED BY CHRIS TURNER

LONDON NEW YORK CALCUTTA

The work is published with the support of the
Publication Assistance Programmes of the Institut français

Seagull Books, 2021

ISBN 978 0 8574 2 739 7

British Library Cataloguing-in-Publication Data
A catalogue record for this book is available
from the British Library

Typeset by Seagull Books, Calcutta, India
Printed and bound by Hyam Enterprises, Calcutta, India

‘Whither thou goest, I will go;
and where thou lodgest, I will lodge: . . .
Where thou diest, will I die, and there will I be buried.’

The Book of Ruth

PART ONE

Claire

CHAPTER 1

Mireille Methuen got married at Dinard on Saturday, 3 February. Claire set off on the Friday. Paul refused to go with her. He hadn't kept up connections with what remained of the family. By eleven o'clock, she was hungry. She was going by the road that ran alongside the River Avre. She preferred to get beyond Breux, Tillières and Verneuil first. After the Verneuil exit, Claire stopped to have lunch at an empty, sandy roadside service area.

The one at Forêt de L'Aigle.

She crossed the car park, heading for a little iron table that stood outside an Alpine chalet. A pot of yellow forsythia had been set down in the middle of the little table. By the pot of forsythia stood a slate on which the day's menu had been chalked. She examined the menu.

A man of around fifty comes shyly out of the inn. He is wearing an apron with big red and white squares on it.

'Can I eat there, in the sun?' Claire points to the little iron table outside.

'You know it isn't twelve yet?'

'Would it be a problem to serve food this early?'

'No.'

'So I'd like to sit there, in this ray of sunshine, even if it isn't noon yet.'

*

The innkeeper doesn't seem to warm to the idea. But at least he makes no reply. He is behaving strangely. He casts a weather eye over Claire. She goes up to him and takes him by the arm. She is twice as tall as he is.

'I'm talking to you: I asked if I can sit over there in the sun.'

'There?

'Yes, there in that ray of sunshine.'

The innkeeper looks up at her with his blue eyes.

'I'd like to eat there, in the sunshine at eleven o'clock on a February morning—even if it's just a salad,' she repeats.

Silence.

'Monsieur, I think you owe me an answer.'

Then the innkeeper goes over and picks up the notice—the slate the day's menu is chalked on—and the bunch of forsythia.

He takes them into the chalet.

He comes back with a sponge.

He slowly wipes the table.

As he wipes it, it becomes clear that it's wobbly.

The innkeeper is on his knees. Roots have lifted the earth. He slips a pebble under one foot of the table.

With one knee still on the floor, raising his eyebrows, he looks up to Claire and says simply: 'I was hesitating because there's a brown owl there.'

He points to the top of the tree.

Both of them raise their heads at the same time.

There's a lightness to the pure blue air.

The oak seems bare, despite the new little leaves caught in the sun's rays.

'I think it'll be sleeping at this time of day,' Claire suggests.

'Do you think so?'

Claire nods.

'Do you really think so?'

The innkeeper, still with one knee on the ground, his arms crossed on the other, regards her quizzically in silence.

'I'm certain of it,' says Claire.

She pulls out the chair, sits down at the little table and begins to cry softly.

*

The wedding guests are to gather at the town hall at ten thirty.

Claire ate breakfast as early as she could (as soon as the hotelkeeper had been to fetch bread from the baker's), at a quarter past seven.

At nine, she goes to the market and roams around.

She examines a punnet of strawberries that are completely out of season. She can't resist taking one, slipping it into her mouth and experiencing its flavour for herself.

She closes her eyes. She tastes.

*

She was tasting a strawberry with little more flavour to it than the water it contained when she heard a voice that moved her with indescribable force. She felt her insides dilate without quite understanding what was happening to her.

She opened her eyes. She turned around.

A little further on, to her left, she saw a woman selling organic vegetables who was in deep discussion with an elderly lady.

She went over to them slowly.

The vegetables on sale weren't very attractive; they had a puny look to them, were shapeless and their skins were deliberately left muddy.

The voice belonged to the tiny lady who was standing in front of them.

Her white hair was tied in a bun; above it, she wore a headscarf—with a pattern of pink flowers on a black background—that was too small for the volume of her hair. The old lady was asking what the leeks were like.

Claire loved this voice she was hearing ten feet away.

She adored this voice.

She tried to put a name to this clear timbre, to these vague rhythmic phrases that were drawing her body to them. The voice rose from among the cos lettuce and the beetroot. It asked suddenly, authoritatively, for a bunch of radishes. When the voice asked for chard, Claire Methuen's eyes filled with tears. And yet she didn't cry, but, with blurred vision, she was unsurprised to see the hand and the ring suddenly loom above the large dark spinach leaves and take the drab recycled-paper bag the vegetable seller was holding out.

*

Claire jostled the people in the queue.

Those waiting their turn began to mutter and moan.

'Madame Ladon,' murmured Claire very quietly.

Nothing. The old lady didn't turn around.

Louder, 'Madame Ladon!'

She saw the old lady's back stiffen and slowly her face turned towards her. The old lady had brown eyes and gold-rimmed glasses. She looked up into Claire's face and seemed very confused to have this tall young woman—twice as tall as she was—call her by name. Madame Ladon didn't recognize Claire immediately. She was looking her up and down when a gentleman in an Alpine hat came over to order Claire back to her place in the queue.

'Madame Ladon,' Claire repeated.

Claire took the shopping bag from the old lady's hands. She put it on the ground. She stroked her fingers, which were so beautiful, so translucent, so well jointed, so wizened. She stroked them one by one, as she used to. The old woman's gaze had softened. Her white hair, fine as it was and tinged with blue, floated freely around her face.

'I don't believe it. You're the Methuen girl?'

Then they stepped away in silence from the queue and the stall.

'You've come back?'

'You too. You've come back to Brittany. Are you back at Saint-Énogat?' asked Claire.

'Indeed I am.'

The stallholder was as emotional as the two women seemed to be—she had a trader's sense of these things. She set aside the second recycled-paper bag, by the scales, the one with the leeks sticking out of it. The radishes were no bigger than gooseberries and much paler.

'You're Marie-Hélène's big sister,' said Madame Ladon softly.

Claire nodded. She was incapable of speech. Her throat had tightened.

'And the youngest?'

'Paul's in Paris.'

'I have to finish my shopping, but promise without fail that you'll come over and see me before you go back.'

'When?'

'Come and see me now at Saint-Énogat, after lunch.'

'I can't. It's Mireille's wedding.'

'It's Philippe Methuen's daughter that's getting married?'

'Yes, Mireille's getting married, but I'll still be here tomorrow.'

'Tomorrow, then. Sunday. After Mass, whenever you like.'

'Still in the same house?'

'Still the same.'

*

It was dark. She had drunk too much wine at the wedding reception. In her hotel room, with the map of the town unfolded on the bed, Claire checked on the road to Madame Ladon's at Saint-Énogat. Then she fell back to sleep.

At nine she breakfasted in her room.

She pushed the armchair over to the window.

She lit a cigarette. With the hotel's phone book open on her lap, she looked up names from her childhood. She found Évelyne's number. The phone rang and rang. She wasn't there and there was no answering machine.

She couldn't find Simon Quelen in the directory.

She did find Fabienne Les Beaussais.

Fabienne answered right away.

'It's Claire, Claire Methuen. Do you remember me?'

'You're mad ringing at this hour, it's Sunday.'

'Do you remember me—Claire Methuen?'

'Yes, of course I do.'

'Did I wake you?'

'Yes.'

'Are you alone?'

'Yes.'

'Well, come and have breakfast with me?'

They arranged to meet right away at the harbour café, La Barque de Festivus, opposite where the shuttle to the islands left from.

Fabienne parked the post-office bicycle on the pavement just beside the table where Claire was already sitting with a cup of coffee.

Claire stood up, but they didn't quite manage to kiss. Their lips grazed each other's cheeks. Fabienne immediately pulled up a chair and sat down beside her.

'That's given you a shock. Your best friend's a post-woman.'

'Why do you say that, Fabienne?'

'When you were little, it was *your* dream to deliver the mail, wasn't it?'

'Not my dream but it's a fine thing to do.'

'And you?'

'Another coffee. Two more coffees, please. Do you want a croissant? Me, I'm still translating.'

'How many languages did you know? You knew ten languages, twenty . . .'

Claire shrugged her shoulders.

'I fancied you might have taken up the piano professionally.'

'I saw Madame Ladon yesterday.'

'Yes, she told me when I went by her house.'

'Do you see her?'

'How could I not? I take her her mail and her newspaper every day. What's the matter? Have you hurt yourself?'

Fabienne reached forward and touched the wound on Claire's jaw.

'It was the wind.'

'They chatted for half an hour about everything and nothing, then fell silent. They looked at each other, the tide went out, the boats keeled over and the tang of the estuary reached them on the wind.

'I have to go,' says Fabienne. 'I won't ask you back. My boyfriend's coming to lunch.'

They got up and walked along the quayside. Fabienne pushed the post-office bicycle all the way along the quay.

'Fabienne?'

'Yes.'

The low quay wall was too damp and cracked for her to put her hand on it.

Claire asked Fabienne: 'Is Simon still here?'

'Yes.'

'I didn't find him in the phone book.'

'You wouldn't. He's moved to La Clarté. He's put a manager in his parents' chemist's shop and taken over the little one on the harbour at La Clarté. He's become mayor of La Clarté too.'

Fabienne added: 'His son's ill. He lives with his wife and his son at Saint-Lunaire.'

'Gwenaëlle?'

'Yes, it makes sense, doesn't it?'

'It does.'

They were standing at the gateway to Dinard beach.

They were both staring at the old wooden helter-skelter, though not seeing it.

Both believed they were speaking, but by now they were no longer speaking to each other.

Fabienne heaved herself into the saddle of her bicycle.

Silently, Claire stared at the empty white air above the sea.

*

She was awakened suddenly. She was on the beach, her back against a rock. A little girl was tapping on her thigh.

'Look!'

The little girl drew herself right up into the face of Claire, who had dozed off.

'I said, look!'

Then she opened her little hands, revealing a pale, translucent crab that immediately ran off between the gaps in her tiny fingers. It fell on to the sand. It tried to dig down into it. It ran diagonally across the furrows in the sand.

The little girl, now on all fours, managed to get it back into the palm of her hand.

'I'm making a crab factory. Look! The water comes in here,' said the little girl, turning her head towards Claire as she pointed to the breakwater where she'd set up her factory.

'You're still asleep!'

The child was tapping Claire again.

'Why have you got really black eyes?'

*

She climbed the rocks one by one. She was walking on the heathland, through the heather, the moss, the broom. She was back in the places of her childhood. She recognized the blocks of granite, the bushes, the paths, the old walls, the steep steps, the sea, the din of the sea. She was eager to rediscover them.

*

To get to La Clarté, if you're coming from Dinard by the coastal path, you have to go by Port-Salut, Port-Riou and Saint-Énogat, then round the new thalasso-therapy centre and up to the top of the hill.

After the Roche Pelée headland, you have to climb again by quite a steep path until you get to the plateau.

From that point on, it gets wilder. This is heathland. At the far end of the plateau are the so-called Pierres

Couchées, the recumbent stones whose location is marked by the chapel of Notre-Dame de la Clarté. It takes two hours to get across the heath and the scrubland. If you go back down, just before you get to Plage-Blanche, if you lean over, you can see the cliff that drops down to the sea but you can't really see the harbour because it's too directly below the chapel to make it out.

The harbour can only be seen from the sea.

And, even from the sea, you can't fully see the village of La Clarté as it clings to the cliffs.

You can just about see the washing drying in the wind.

You can see the satellite dishes.

You can just about make out, if you know them, the ancient, black, granite houses, stacked in their terraces, partly buried in the cliff, held in place by the stairways cut out of the granite—dark exhausting stairways with innumerable high steps.

*

Standing motionless on the cliff, her body exposed to wind and sky, she is happy again.

She listens to the sea down below.

She closes her eyes.

Then gradually, far off in the distance, in the depths of her being, she can hear the porcelain cistern that noisily poured water into the earthenware bowl in her aunt's bedroom. The bucket of water one filled in the sink by pulling out the bit of wood that closed off the black rubber tube which came from the cistern up above the roof of the farm.

The noise of her aunt 'Guite—Marguerite Methuen, her father's sister-in-law—holding the coffee-mill between her thighs and milling the beans. Then the noise of the axe striking the log to chop firewood, the noise of the billhook cutting furze. Her cousins were much older than she was. They went to cut and bind it beside the river. The elder of her cousins, Philippe Methuen, was Mireille's father. He'd taken over the farm. As a child, she watched them make their bundles of firewood. They never let her take part in the work they did. She'd watch them with great curiosity. They were already working on the farm. They couldn't stand her because she was brilliant at school, because she was a girl, because their mother always protected her. Paul, her little brother, was a boarder at Pontorson. They only saw him in the summer holidays. Only in the summer holidays, in August, did they have to put up with his whining

*

Now it's another noise jingling inside her. She's making holes in shells, in hundreds of shells. She runs a red thread through them. She made little bells out of snail shells. She cut up cardboard cartons for water and beer bottles and stuck them together with flour paste. She made houses for her snails, for her grasshoppers, for her frogs, for her caterpillars.

She watched with a kind of uninterrupted thrill as her caterpillars turned into butterflies.

Lastly, in the depths of her memory, for a split second she glimpsed eight dirty cows standing in a red lorry in a downpour, being washed by the rain; eight cows streaming with rainwater, a car whose engine had burned out, itself drenched by the rain, a car that had smashed into the guardrail of the cliff.

She made nests for fallen blackbirds and prepared little meals of bread and milk for them in the hope they would survive.

CHAPTER 2

She walked on past the Pierres Couchées and began the descent. It had always been dizzying and still was. She began slowly to descend the hundreds of steps that ran down sheer to the sea. She was careful not to lean over. However, despite the feeling of vertigo, and though she wasn't trying to see them, she glimpsed the little fishing boats coming back into harbour far below.

She saw the launch leaving for Saint-Malo, pursued by gulls.

The trawler waited for the launch to pass.

Its wake ceased to be visible as soon as it came into the channel.

The seagulls abandoned their pursuit of the island shuttle and came back to it.

Further on was the little cylindrical white lighthouse atop its little white tower that marked La Clarté harbour.

*

Once she'd reached the bottom, everything, seen from below, was small, much less anxious-making and less invisible. You looked up and there was an old harbour town built on several levels and sheltered from bandits, customs men, the English, pirates, police, the Germans, the Normans and the wind. The house frontages along the quayside were extremely narrow. There was one shop after another, each having the benefit of only a single window. The baker's didn't even have a window and, as soon as it was dry, a stall was set up outside with folded pancakes and two-pound loaves for sale. The blue neon light of the harbour café stood above an entirely glass door. Then came the high-class shoe shop, the newsagent-and-tobacconist's, and lastly the little stairway that led up to the presbytery and, subsequently, broadened out into the twelve steps of La Clarté church.

The chemist's was on the corner with the post office, in front of the little block of flats in the Ruelle des Degrés-du-Marché.

The grille was down.

The shop was closed.

Above the quay were stacked in successive terraces or arrayed in little squares at the top of the stairways the thirty or forty old, slate-roofed houses, all nestling in the cliff side and reaching almost half-way up it.

All the streets were flights of stairs. No car, moped, bicycle, tricycle or skateboard could negotiate them. It was the quietest village there was. With not even the sound of a lawnmower. No garden had enough space to stretch out in, nor enough earth to root its bushes. Hence, at almost all the windows were window boxes, little wisterias, winter hyacinths, old geraniums, pansies.

There were said to be seven hundred steps in total in the port of La Clarté, if you went up as far as the Pierres Couchées and the Notre-Dame chapel.

Few people ventured to do so.

For shopping, it was better to go down to the harbour. Or you waited for market day. Or you took the shuttle and went to make your purchases in Saint-Malo, Cancale or, nearer to hand, Saint-Briac or Dinard.

*

She leaves. She steps up on to the gangway and boards the launch which drops her off outside the La Gonelle restaurant at Dinard marina.

She crosses the beach again. She takes the coastal path as far as Saint-Énogat. The tide is coming in. It's a spring tide. At new moon, seen now in the emptiness of the night sky, the sea fashions the highest waves of the month. This is the point when the—choppier—incoming tide unleashes the foamiest waves and the sea's noise is at its most deafening. The waves explode far below Claire, but they spatter her face, hurling spume up over her hood which keeps falling down her back. She follows the concrete path, the force of the wind making her run, it being so difficult simply to walk in this squall.

Her hood won't hold. The wind whips up her blonde hair, standing it on end like a damp yellow torch. She deliberately heads into the wind, continuing to press on as fast as possible.

She arrives at Madame Ladon's soaked to the skin.

*

She spent two hours at Madame Ladon's, called a taxi, came back to the hotel, picked up her things, paid at reception, got back in the taxi, went back to Madame Ladon's and stayed there for four days.

Then she went back to Paris.

Then she took ten days' holiday.

She spent those ten days at Saint-Malo in the flat of a friend of Madame Ladon's, a woman who only used it in the summer. She went once a day to Madame Ladon's either for lunch or dinner. For next to nothing, she hired an old Renault 4 which she left, when she took the train to Paris, in the parking area at the harbour station.

CHAPTER 3

She's at Versailles. She's in the garden.

Despite the foliage of the big bay tree, the loamy earth is getting a little of the light the sun gives off.

Along the low wall, hidden by the cement edging that holds back the earth, in a little gully of mud, near the boxwood ball, she glimpses two little petals of a red primrose trying to haul itself up towards the pools of disparate light that open up between the branches and the leaves.

A little islet of light spreads on the moss which is being eaten by a wonderful little snail.

Claire crouches down to the little snail and murmurs to it: 'We should replant trees. We should cut the branches of the bay tree. We should saw off the big branch that I always keep bumping into. We should replant flowers. We should dig over the earth. This is just the moment to re-seed a nice green lawn.' But the snail is reluctant to answer. It prods its head forward a moment, then retracts it into its shell. Claire feels water running gently and copiously along her back. She gets up. She discovers her entire body is covered in sweat. Even her belly is covered in sweat. Anxiety is such an old companion. It isn't perhaps the easiest of companions in this world, but it's a good counsellor. The tightening throat is a cruel, tiresome old sprite, but an impressive reader of the cards that time deals. Claire never takes anxiety on frontally any more. She's too well aware of its stratagems and dizzying effects.

She takes the empty paint pot in one hand and with the other drags the dirty tarpaulin to the dustbins.

Then Claire slowly walks back up the avenue of handsome Versailles villas.

She fastens the padlock on the chain around the bars of the gate.

Then she goes back down the lane, being careful, in her high-heeled shoes, not to slip on the moss and paving stones. She leaves the lane with gathering energy. She suddenly looks around in dismay at all these fine villas, all these magnificent little houses that seem like tawdry constructs—things of plaster, matchwood and reminiscences. The flowerpots on the little balconies are pathetic. The big daffodils, newly bought, are too bulky and brightly coloured. They look as though they're made of plastic. They don't even bend in the wind.

*

She leans her hair against the pane of the train window.

The cool air flows through it.

She's on the high-speed train to Saint-Malo.

She looks out at the countryside, the fields, the hedges, the herds and flocks, the ponds.

She looks at the mistletoe that is throttling the little old oak trees that mark off the ditches running round the fields.

Suddenly, she gets up. She goes over to the businessman who is speaking into his mobile phone, a little further along the corridor.

'Excuse me.'

'Yes?'

'Are you able to speak more quietly?'

'Yes.'

'Then try to.'

The businessman gets up and takes his telephone off to the end of the carriage and the toilets.

*

In the car park, she opens the door of the Renault 4 which is covered in a fine layer of dust.

She slows down at a point where the river merges with the bay.

She stops the car gently on the grass.

She gets out.

She looks at the liquid, streaming brilliance of the light thrown on to the rocks beside the immense white sea.

She sees Saint-Malo in the distance.

She can see as far as the Ile de Cézembre.

She walks through the oats and the bracken.

Claire is holding her high-heeled shoes in her hand. She is filled with joy, for joy returned as soon as she saw the bay and glimpsed the tidal power station. She is immediately brimful of glee. She pitches her long bare legs into the new spring grass. The wet air hits her on her forehead, her nose, her cheeks, the back of her hands.

*

She walks for a long time in silence.

*

When she gets back, the sea is high.

She can't get back across the rocks to the car.

She has to go by the road. She leans down. She slips her feet into her shoes. She walks on the tarmac to get back to the car park.

She walks on the mixture of grass and gravel that runs beside the tarmacked road.

Beyond this, the sea is white.

Rain is falling slowly on her.

A dark brown duffle-coat that's too short, a hood that sticks up, two bare knobbly knees—that's Claire.

*

On Sunday, 29 April 2007, the weather was mild. Paul came for the weekend. They were able to eat outside. They ate dinner, face to face, to the sound of hulls and masts bumping together. They'd gone down to the marina at Dinard. The air was just a little cool. Claire explained to Paul why she'd perhaps stay here for a short while. Could he lend her a little money?

'Yes.'

Would he buy something here?

'Certainly not.'

She smiled.

'What about your work?' asked Paul.

'I can do it anywhere,' Claire replies. 'I can deliver it in written form. That's not the problem.'

'What is the problem?'

'I'm tired of being needed.'

'Isn't that a good thing?'

'I'm sick of being useful.'

'God!'

Then they fell silent.

They had both grown up in the bay of the Rance, but not side by side. They had never spent more than a month in summer together—every summer. When their parents had died, when her father, her mother and Lena had died, Claire was nine years old, Paul four. Paul was just a little boy she could neither play with nor talk to, who cried over the tiniest thing, who had abandoned himself to his destiny, whom she looked down on. Then she'd been taken from her uncle after her aunt died, and they'd been put into the care of the local authority. She looked after Paul in the summer, dressed him, taught him languages. She had married very early in life, as soon as she could, so as to gain her freedom. She'd had two daughters who had stayed with their father after she'd divorced him. She'd left the family home just after the birth of the last, Juliette. Juliette was six days old when she'd left. Paul hadn't even known her two little girls. So Paul and Claire barely knew each other. They called each other on 17 May and 26 August for their birthdays, for their saints' days on 29 June for Paul and 11 August for Claire and, lastly, at midnight on New Year's Eve. Five times a year and that was all.

*

The Atlantic crab, usually called *tourteau*, her aunt 'Guite used to call by the local name *houvet*.

She moves her glass of white wine on the white tablecloth.

This is the rapturous *houvet* moment.

She smashes the claws. She tries to break the crab in half, she tears it apart noisily. She gets inside the crab, imagines life beneath the water, a perilous life in the rocky clefts, a life lived deep in darkness, beneath the seaweed, in the noisy, turbulent blackness of the sea. She is happy. She has, herself, the domed forehead of the *houvet*. Stubborn, head down, she pushes her domed shell beneath the seaweed, she reaches out her claws towards the little fishes as they dart by, the slippery grasses, the sea-horses as they rise.

When she is shelling a crab, you no longer hear the sound of her voice.

So happy is she inside her crab that she's no longer of this world.

CHAPTER 4

Paul went back to Paris the next morning—Monday morning—by the first train. It was Claire who dropped him off at the station.

From the TGV high-speed train station, Claire drove out south through Saint-Servan and parked in the marketplace at Dinard. The bookshop was open. She pushed open the door. The place smelt of paint.

'We're closed, it's Monday!' shouted a man from the back of the shop who was painting a shelf.

Claire introduced herself. Évelyne wasn't there. This was a friend of hers who had come to do some painting. He was called Yann. He taught German at the lycée. Yann took off his glasses and said, 'It's Monday, she's gone to Rennes. She's away for the whole day.'

'To Rennes?'

She stared at him, not knowing what to do.

'So you're the language genius?' asked Yann.

She shrugged her shoulders. He spoke to her in German. She replied in German.

Yann said in Breton, 'I'll tell her you called.'

She replied in Breton: 'Never mind, it's not important.'

'Don't shut the door!'

*

Fabienne is walking through the ploughed clods of earth, in the field itself. Claire is walking beside the prickly bushes. Noëlle prefers the tarmacked surface of the road, keeping her feet dry; she's carrying the paper bag full of sandwiches bought at the baker's on the Place Jules-Verne.

Évelyne, walking above them, jumping from rock to rock, is carrying the drinks in her backpack.

You can see the little necks of the bottles sticking up above Évelyne's shoulders.

All four of them are crossing the heath above Saint-Énogat. It's an interminable walk.

There's no one around.

During the week, the paths are empty.

The fields, copses, gardens, villas, roads, paths and heathland—all are still and empty.

Claire is sitting down now. She shakes her blonde head to decline a drink. She isn't thirsty. Noëlle drinks her beer straight from the bottle. Évelyne explains that Gwenaëlle stopped working at the chemist's two years back, because of their child's problems. She explains that he can't count or read.

'He's fine playing with cubes, but jigsaws are beyond him.'

'Oh!' says Fabienne Les Beaussais, who seems very upset.'

They empty the Thermos flask, the remains of the coffee, onto the heathland grass.

They stay sitting on the grass.

All is silent.

There aren't any grasshoppers yet, or butterflies, cicadas or bees. In a way, it's the silence of those creatures they can hear. There's no wind. All is emptiness.

Silently, the clouds rip open one after the other, allowing more and more light to shine through.

And that light floods the heath.

*

She loved this place. She loved the air—so clear that everything was closer. She loved the air—so sharp that sounds were clearer. She felt the need to recognize all of what she had lived through. She sensed the need to recognize all of what she had discovered of the world here in the past. And gradually she did indeed remember everything—names, places, farms, streams, woods. She never tired of walking the streets; of observing the frontages; of rediscovering the houses, the gardens, the little thickets with their species so varied, the brambles of all kinds, the hedges, ditches, copses; of climbing on the blocks of granite; of looking at the wild flowers, the seaweed beds, the rocks, the birds. She loved this country. She loved this shore, fiercely steep and black as it was and going straight up to the sky. She loved this sea.

*

She spun round suddenly. She dashed back across the road. She opened the door without ringing or knocking. She shouted: 'I've come back for my cagoule. I left it on the chair.'

She heard Madame Ladon shouting down from the first floor: 'You'd leave your head if it wasn't screwed on?'

'Well, it was just my anorak!'

She mumbles: 'Goodbye, Madame Ladon.'

*

'Goodbye Madame Ladon!' shouted Madame Andrée.

'Goodbye, Andrée,' yelled Madame Ladon.

The front door slammed.

In the evenings, as soon as the front door slammed, Madame Ladon got up without allowing another second to pass and, with a halting but determined tread, headed for the kitchen.

Madame Ladon always had to wait until Madame Andrée, her cleaning lady, had gone.

'You can come down!' she shouted up the stairs to Claire, who was busy on the first floor typing a translation on her laptop.

Madame Ladon would open the fridge. She would grab a bottle of Muscadet de Liré. She would fill the crystal glasses she had set out on the tray. From the fridge she also took sprigs of little cherry tomatoes. She rolled a dozen of them into a transparent ramekin.

'Where are the sesame breadsticks?' asked Claire.

'Right there in front of you.'

'Where?'

'There, under your nose. I value Andrée greatly, she's a treasure, but you wouldn't believe how impatient I can be for her to leave.'

Madame Ladon had begun to chop gruyere cheese into little pieces.

She suddenly raised her knife.

She pointed it in Claire's direction.

'There isn't enough wine for this evening. Go down to the cellar. There must be some of Monsieur Ladon's Chablis left. I think we're entitled to some Chablis this evening.

Madame Ladon lifted the tray cautiously.

'Let me carry it,' said Claire.

'My dear, we've no more wine. See to the wine. I can't go down to the cellar with my bad leg.'

'Right.'

'Take a candle with you.'

Claire got a candle from the sideboard and a box of matches from up by the gas cooker. She guarded the flame with her hand. She went down into the damp, earthy cold of the cellar.

She came back up with three bottles of Chablis.

'You need an electric light in your cellar, Madame Ladon. The steps are very steep.'

'I've always thought that, but Monsieur Ladon didn't want it. He said it wasn't the thing to do. He claimed the wine had to lie in the dark.'

'I'll take care of it,' said Claire.

*

It was evening. A fine rain rapped against the bay window.

'I've made you a razor clam soup.'

'I can't stay for dinner.'

'You can't stay for dinner?'

'No, I'll just have an aperitif with you and I'm going home.'

'Why?'

'You said lunch *or* dinner. Not both.'

'That's true. I remember saying that,' agreed Madame Ladon. 'It's absurd. I was wrong. Really, I was.'

She looks up at Claire who is standing in the bay window smoking, holding the French window half-open.

'Claire, I've had another idea. Tomorrow is Ascension Day. My friend always comes for the first week in July. Look in your diary. See what day that is.'

'The first of July's a Sunday.'

'Then she'll get here on the Saturday.'

'The 30th of June?'

'That's right. You'll have to give me back the flat you're in and tidy everything up. I'll send Andrée to clean it out.'

'I don't need Andrée. I'll take care of it myself.'

'No matter. Sort it out between you. What I want to say right now, before you go to any trouble and start looking for something, is that I'd like you to go and see Monsieur Ladon's farm.'

'I didn't know you had a farm. I never imagined you as a farmer's wife.'

'I never go there.'

'Where is it?'

'On the Saint-Lunaire plateau. Do you know the plateau up on the heath?'

'Yes, very well. I know the heath, but there's nothing there.'

'Don't you believe it. They're very well-hidden buildings.'

'But where?'

'Behind the Pierres Couchées and the little chapel of Notre Dame de La Clarté, above the harbour.'

'Above the old harbour at La Clarté?'

'Yes, but above the clifftops. Almost in the middle of the heath. Half a mile before La Tremblaie farm.'

'I can't think where that is.'

'I'll show you. You can take me in your new car.'

'You can't get on to the clifftop by car.'

'Then we'll walk.'

'You know, we go and picnic there occasionally at lunchtime, with Noëlle, Fabienne Les Beaussais and Évelyne. It goes on forever. You have to walk a long, long way.'

'I'm quite able to walk. At least I can walk when I force my leg to do my bidding. As I recall, there's a little wood of filbert trees.'

'Yes, there is a little hazel wood there.'

'The farm's hidden in that wood. Or, rather, it nestles in it. That farm is what the Ladon family dumped on me in exchange for the beautiful apartment in Toulon. Listen, my dear, go and see first with Andrée. Have a look, both of you, to see if it can be sorted out.

If it's habitable. At least for summer. See what needs doing to it. I'll warn you, it isn't luxurious. It's an old-style farm. Anyway, go see and tell me what you think of it. If it's too run down, I'll have to take the decision to sell it. You tell me.'

'Yes, I'll tell you.'

Madame Ladon opens the drawer under the low table.

'Look, here's the key.'

Claire takes the big iron key in her hand.

*

At dawn, the bells ring. They peal out loudly. It's Ascension Day. She sees the big key she placed on her bedside table when she came in. She calls Paul.

'Happy Birthday, Paul dearest.'

'You woke me up.'

'I hope I'm the first. You're forty-two years old. Love and kisses.'

She switches off her mobile. Her brother doesn't have the time to answer.

*

Madame Ladon comes back from evening Mass. Claire has set out the aperitifs and is waiting for her. She closes the French window.

'Madame Ladon, can I ask you a question?'

'Yes, my dear, of course.'

'Why don't you have a piano any more?'

'You noticed?'

'A grand piano is something you notice.'

'Come and see what I have instead.'

She takes her to the back of the room, by the French window. There are several papyrus plants in big planished copper pots. In the middle, where the grand piano used to stand, a table is turned towards the garden. There's a scented candle, an empty teacup, a pile of seven or eight DVDs. And in the middle, a DVD player.

'When I'm alone, I watch films. Two a day. One performance at two p.m. Another at eight.'

She takes the little pile from the table.

'My hands were too painful to bring the piano back here. My fingers wouldn't go where I wanted them to any more. They lagged behind my brain. They lagged behind the song I hoped to hear them produce. I'm much happier with my films. I'd even say I'm very happy. I get some from the local library too. The new releases that interest me I buy from a shop in Saint-Malo, near the hospital. To tell the truth, though, I very often watch my favourites over again.'

'What are your favourite DVDs, Madame Ladon?' asks Claire.

'Come and see.'

The two of them launch into discussion of their favourite films, favourite posters, favourite images and favourite stars.

*

'I live a very ordered life. In the morning at nine, when I get the mail from Fabienne, I read the newspaper. At eleven o'clock, leg permitting, I go shopping. Otherwise, it's Andrée who takes care of that. At any rate, Andrée comes every day at eleven. I have my lunch in front of the TV. I rest a bit. The first film show is two p.m. I garden. Well, actually, I walk round my garden because I can't squeeze the two arms of the secateurs any more. I deadhead the roses with my fingers, which isn't a good way to do it. Then I heat the water for my tea. I listen to music on Monsieur Ladon's record player. Then, at last, it's aperitif time. Hotly awaited. I have dinner. Second film show at eight. Then I get myself ready for bed.'

*

'I won't ask you to stay to dinner tonight, Claire my dear, as I'm a little tired.'

'Don't worry, I'm not staying.'

'When that's the case, I prefer to be alone a little. It's a holiday tomorrow. Whitsun. Do you like to be alone, Claire?'

Claire is standing there, enormous, ever more tanned, ever blonder, towering over the tiny, shrunken, pale Madame Ladon in her orange, tub-style easy chair.

She thinks . . .

'Take your time, my darling.'

'I don't really know, Madame Ladon.'

'Then forget my silly question.'

Claire goes over to the open French window. 'I know that I hated being an orphan and I hated living together. I couldn't bear to live under my husband's rule and the demands of my two daughters. Having said that, I don't really know if I like living alone. I think I force myself to believe I do.'

'I don't force myself!' exclaimed Madame Ladon behind her. 'It was a real discovery! I dearly love being alone. Understand, Claire, I don't say that because I don't want you to have dinner with me every night or don't want you to come and live here with me, but I absolutely love these periods of silence when my life is my own. Up until the last day of his life, my husband imposed his timetable on me, his affection, his concerns, his plans, his fears. It's incredible when I think about it: I adored widowhood from the first. I hadn't remotely foreseen how much I'd appreciate solitude. It wasn't any effort. I watched it happening as though I were a spectator. To my great astonishment, my mourning turned into a holiday. I respected my husband's qualities and his anxiety, his honesty and his piety; I suddenly had a break from his torment. It wasn't just a holiday but an enormous holiday. I still feel the same way. I left everything we'd acquired at Toulon to the four children he had before we married. I came back here with nothing—just myself. Everything here is mine alone. Even that old farm on the Saint-Énogat plateau, which belonged to his parents, is mine alone. You know, the farm I gave you the key to the other day. Up on the heathland by La Tremblaie farm. Have you actually been to take a look?'

'No.'

'When I was widowed, I chose to get ahead of the game on everything to do with my husband's will, so as not to owe them anything. I'll tell you the truth: it was so that I'd never have to see them again.'

Madame Ladon closes her eyes.

Claire has closed the French window. She has come back over to Madame Ladon. She has reached forward over the low table. She puts the glasses, the bottle, the ramekins, the rest of the cherry tomatoes and the breadsticks on the tray.

Mme Ladon, her eyes closed, is speaking very softly:

'The local people called the farm above there La Tremblaie because of the trees called *trembles*—aspens. My father-in-law used to say it had been a place of worship because the aspen used to be called the fever tree. This is what they had to do. The person with the fever would cut the bark with his knife. He'd put his mouth to the sap that flowed from the cut, though he wouldn't drink it. He'd just place his lips on the cut he'd made, blowing on it very hard. Then, coughing very hard on to the sap, the sick man would say: "Tremble and shiver more than I'm doing." Then the fever would pass straight into the tree and its leaves would begin to tremble. That meant the illness had left the body.'

'Did it work?'

'As well as antibiotics. But you had to beware of addiction!'

CHAPTER 5

The water in the ponds was growing dark. There was a rosy tint on the heath. Claire had preferred to go alone to see the farm. Alone so that she could make up her mind for herself. She didn't want to hear anyone else's opinion or be constrained in her own feelings by the look on anyone else's face. Another day, she would ask Madame Ladon's cleaner, Madame Andrée, to go with her. She turned right and went past the Pony Club.

She went along by Villa Géhan.

She went past the pillbox.

Once up among the bushes, ponds and the tall grasses on the heath, she got lost.

*

Dusk was beginning to fall when she discovered where she was.

You couldn't see any clear path on the ground now. To put it even more simply, the path leading to the old farm had faded away beneath the grass. She found a little wooden sign still hanging round the trunk of a tree—a hazel tree, in fact—held on with wire. It hadn't occurred to her that the farm might be quite so invisible on the plateau—even to the eyes of hikers. She left the car beside the hazel tree with the notice on it. There were too many potholes, too many little pools of water and too much grass to be able to drive any further. She locked the four car doors. She walked for a while in the long oats, scratching her ankles on the brambles. She walked through what was a real wood of hazel trees and undergrowth surrounding the little farm buildings.

It was tiny, silent, entrancing and damp.

The farmhouse had been built, long ago, to be sheltered from the wind, in the bottom of a hollow and with its back to a little wood protecting it from all the squalls that blew off the sea.

A shed roof, a sheet of corrugated iron, lay on the floor, leaning against a workbench and singing intermittently.

There was a little farmyard that had turned into meadow, a large half-dead orchard, a big pond near the fence, surrounded by a semi-circle of tall, hardy reeds.

And the remains of a dung heap between the pond and the steps up to the house. In addition to the farm, there was a stable, a woodshed, a lean-to and a cow byre.

She went into the orchard which was full of dead branches. Two cherry trees, a wall of pears, three tiny peach trees, a fig tree doubtless protected from frost by a sort of well covered by a blackberry bush and connected to the pond by a little runnel, and a mirabelle plum tree.

She recognized the trees of her childhood.

Looking at the leaves on the branches, she could imagine the fruits.

Little by little, night was falling.

The light here was very brown, the soil being so soaked. The ground was curiously bumpy on account of the water pouring down, or rather winding its way towards this hollow. Water that stagnated there or formed little paths that ended in all these little ponds with their mosquitos, frogs and slugs. The trees, the roots of the brambles and the white willow plantation surrounding the main pond couldn't soak up all the water that came, no doubt, as much from the sea spray as from the rains. So they all grew together in a great vault of leaves, affording the place wonderful coolness in summer but a grim dampness in autumn.

Claire walked along, paying no attention to the hosts of snails whose shells cracked suddenly beneath the soles of her shoes.

In the shed, what must have been a pre-First World War cart was crumbling away with its shafts in the air.

In the pigsty, beside some empty troughs, piles of logs were covered in fungi; there was a store of coal nuts and mountains of wine bottles, their contents drained and the bottles simply piled up.

The key Madame Ladon had given her revolved loosely in the lock when she inserted it.

She pushed.

The farmhouse door stayed closed.

Claire tried to see between the big wooden shutters, but dampness and sea salt kept them stuck to the facade of the building. Claire shook them and they began to give a little. She managed to pull them free and opened a first one. She looked on the ground for a pebble. Cautiously, she broke the pane of the window to the right of the catch, knocked out the fragments of glass, slid in her hand, raised the catch, opened the two sides of the window, pulled herself up, climbed in through the window and found herself in a large, very low-ceilinged kitchen.

On the left was an enormous fireplace.

An old cast-iron cooker had been placed inside it.

Some ten black pans hung above her head.

Claire quickly passed through the kitchen, and walked rapidly through an empty, smaller low room, a sort of mud room where there was nothing to be seen, and climbed the stairs. At least she tried to climb the stairs, but her knees gave way.

She had to sit down on a step for a moment.

She had to get out, running as fast as she could, jumping through the window.

It was a moment of panic that drove her out.

*

She found herself outside, feeling hollow and empty, sitting in the grass by the pond, her belly soaked with sweat, chock-full of anxiety.

*

It was darkest night. It was cold. She stood up and looked to the sky. Many dense dark clouds were passing overhead.

*

Inexplicably, she couldn't find her way again in the darkness. When she tried to get back to the hazel tree with the sign on it and find her car, she got lost once more among the brambles, bracken, broom, gorse and pools of water. She wandered around on the heath. She saw a light in the distance. She went towards it in the darkness. It was La Tremblaie farm.

*

As they were talking together beneath a naked light-bulb in the farmyard, the La Tremblaie farmer caught a passing hen and wrung its neck. He took it to the kitchen. Turning around, he called Claire to come into the kitchen with him.

'Take a chair,' he said, when she was in the room.

But Claire preferred to stand in the farmhouse kitchen.

When she had been taken in, long ago, by her father's brother, she had lived on a farm, the big Pont Touraude farm that was home to her appalling cousins. It was on the Rance estuary, beyond Le Minihac-sur-Rance, near the lock. She had lived there for five years.

The La Tremblaie farmer went back out into the yard, ran off after another hen, lifted it off the ground by its neck and tightened his hands around it.

'Will you stay and have dinner, Madame Ladon?'

'Madame Methuen. My name's Claire Methuen. No, of course not. I really don't want to put you to any trouble. I just want to find my way again.'

'I'm happy to have you stay.'

'All right, then.'

'I know a Philippe Methuen who's a farmer like me, over beyond La Marquerais.'

'He's my first cousin. I was the niece of Armel and 'Guite Methuen of Pont Touraude.'

'That's him.'

He held out his hand.

'The name's Calève, Henri Calève, but you can call me Old Man Calève, the way everyone else does.'

He took Claire's hand and held it in his own at some length.

'Are you going to take over the Ladon farm?'

'Yes.'

She pulled back her hand.

'Just to live there?'

'What do you mean?'

'A Methuen moving into the Ladon farm—are you not going to farm the land?'

'No, just live there.'

'That's a relief. I wouldn't have liked to see competition arriving.'

'I'm not competition. I won't even raise a hen. I won't even have a rabbit hutch.'

'Not even a goldfish.'

'Not even a jar with a goldfish in it.'

'Let's drink to the arrival of my new neighbour.'

He goes and fetches two little glasses. He fills them with wine.

'You know, I can do the hens tomorrow. This evening is soup time. Are you OK with soup?'

'I'm OK with soup.'

'We'll have soup, some eggs, cheese, coffee, biscuits and brandy, and afterwards I'll take you to your car.'

'Thank you, Monsieur Calève.'

'My pleasure, Madame Methuen. How do you like your eggs?'

'Hard boiled.'

*

Old Man Calève put the coffee pot back down on the table. He slid his hand on to the oilcloth, filled his palm with crumbs and swallowed them down. He got up.

'Let's go.'

They drove for a short time in the night beneath dense scudding clouds.

On the heath, by the corner of a field of maize, stood the shell of a Citroen lorry.

'Look!'

'I can't see anything. It's too dark.'

'Take a good look at that shell of an old Citroen lorry. Can you see it?'

'Yes.'

'With that as a way-marker, you won't go wrong when you're heading to your farm.'

CHAPTER 6

Wednesday is market day at La Clarté.

It is raining violently but the quayside and the stairways are teeming with people.

Claire pushes open the door of the chemist's. There are two people waiting.

He looked up.

She remained still. She was staring at him.

He saw her, recognized her, abruptly lowered his eyes. On the counter near the cash register, his hand, as it was holding the prescription, began to shake.

She turned around suddenly and left immediately, because she too had begun to tremble all over.

*

She would have liked to run. It was raining stair-rods. It was June in Brittany. It was virtually impossible to cross the little square. The whole population, umbrellas in hand, little see-through plastic headscarves over hair, bare pates tucked away under woolly hats, were doing their shopping on the stairways, crowding the side streets and terraces, standing around on the quayside at La Clarté.

*

She manages to get through the thronging mass. Her hair is soaking wet. She is crying unrestrainedly because no one can see she is crying with the violent rain falling. She goes over towards the landing stage for the shuttle boat. She just buys some rubber ankle boots as she waits for the launch that serves the islands.

*

It is dark. She is walking by the waterside. She is no longer at La Clarté, but has just left the marina at Dinard. She passes beneath Fabienne's windows. All the lights are out. Reaching the Grand-Rue, she feels that she's up to climbing it. She goes up the street. A café is open. She hesitates. There are people there, gathered in a circle, watching a match on the TV. She doesn't want noise. So she goes back down. She walks along the Promenade du Clair de Lune, past the lock, and gets to the moonlit beach. She is happy she made the decision to come back here. She is happy to be in Brittany. She is happy to walk among the rocks with the sound of the sea in her ears.

*

It is eight o'clock in the morning. The school bell is ringing at Saint-Lunaire. Her domed forehead is pressed against the car window. Gwenäelle Quelen comes down the Grand-Rue with Simon's son. Gwenäelle is slim and as perfect and ravishing as ever. The boy is her spitting image. He is strangely, impassively handsome. He is taller than the other children. He is calmer. He holds his mother's hand through the railings, while the other children around him are screaming. He has pale eyes. He has a very handsome, sad face.

The bell rings for the children to go in.

Claire is looking now at the children forming into rows in the playground down below her.

Suddenly the shouts fade to a murmur.

The children go into the class rooms.

There is silence.

*

The playground is empty.

There is just an oblique ray of sunshine dividing the silent playground in two, casting light on the red bricks of the main wall.

Gwenäelle isn't there any more. Claire gets out of the car. It is spitting with rain.

She takes a walk in the drizzle.

*

Then she leaves Saint-Lunaire. She goes to the three Pierres Couchées and the chapel. She drives up on to the heath.

The sky was entirely blue.

The wind was coming off the sea.

The tiny chapel Notre-Dame de La Clarté stood in the middle of the field with the Pierres Couchées. These were three large recumbent menhirs at the top of the cliff. In Brittany, a great many fields of Neolithic stones were rechristened Notre-Dame de La Clarté. This word *clarté* transmitted the old meaning of a form of worship in which the rising of the sun and the sudden return of spring were both celebrated.

She leaves the old Renault 4 in the car park. She slips under the barbed wire.

She walks across the field of oats.

She goes across the heath, but she doesn't head towards the farm at all.

She goes off through the field of mustard, down the rue de l'Anse-au-Genêt—Broom Cove Street—and on down to Plage-Blanche—White Beach—to see the waves come rolling in.

The wind turns round in the cove.

The waves are very high and brown.

They fritter away into the air as they roll in.

*

Two little girls were playing at the edge of the tideline.

The brown waves whipped up white droplets that fell on them with all the force of the swirling wind.

The air, whisking water from the tops of the waves, soaked their cheeks and foreheads.

They were shrieking with joy. Gleaming with sea spray, they ran in all directions and danced, letting themselves be blown, like the waves, by a wind that was going in all directions.

Later, further along the shoreline, they went to sit with a man sitting flanked by two motionless dogs.

*

Claire reached the salt meadows, where her feet sank deep into the earth.

Even when freighted with mud and seashells, her new boots were well made for marching on the foreshore and among the lowest rocks. They didn't slip off her ankles. They were comfortable. She walked for a long time. Her tracksuit bottoms were heavy with grass dampened by dew and sea. She crossed the road and took the 'Lumière Brothers' hiking trail.

*

She came back slowly by car, in first gear, along the path full of potholes and puddles with a carton of water bottles, some cleaning products, floorcloths, a pack of four dishcloths—yellow, green, red and blue—a roll of bin bags, sponges and buckets.

At the farm, Madame Andrée had opened all the windows. She had already taken out some mouldy clothes, some old moth-eaten carpets, some curtains full of dust which she piled up in a cart.

By the steps at the front of the house stood four big black bin bags that were already full.

On the steps: a dark blue woolly hat with a splendid shiny peak, rolls of chewing tobacco wrapped in yellow paper, empty ornate perfume bottles.

'Can I take them, Madame Methuen?'

'Of course you can, Madame Andrée.'

*

In the farm kitchen, Claire, on her knees by the dresser, pulls out a Puff Billiards game. She pulls out two rubber puffers that are dried, cracked and unusable.

Madame Andrée, sitting at the table, is sorting the crockery.

After she's emptied the lower half of the dresser, Claire goes off to the low room next to the kitchen (Claire called it the mudroom; Madame Andrée used the dialect word *cafourotte*). On all fours on the tiled floor, she pulls out from beneath the stairs two flippers, a pair of goggles, a demijohn, three little water-skins, an iron flask, road maps, school textbooks, a plaster mould and some children's board games.

A little railway signal that still works.

A tinplate sailing boat that rolls along on little wheels.

Her palms are sweaty.

On the tiled floor, she gives the tinplate sailing boat on little wheels a push and it rolls along.

*

She brakes, mounts the verge and stops the Renault by the lock. She lifts the barbed wire that runs round Uncle Armel's field.

She leans over but is too tall to get under it. Once again, she's forced to get down on all fours. Almost on her stomach, she slips under the barbed wire without tearing her anorak. She climbs the hill to the tree that stands alone at the top of the field. Once upon a time, that was a vantage point for watching the road to La Ville. She sees the place again. She tries to reconstruct the landscape as it was when she was small. There were so few cars then, the horses came directly across the fields. You could be there an hour and see no one.

She drives up the coast.

She brakes.

She crosses the narrow bridge at La Bardelière.

She puts her foot down. She drives rapidly past the farm that is now in cousin Philippe's hands. She's keen to take a look at everything, to take it all in at a terrified glance, but her courage fails her.

PART TWO

Simon

CHAPTER 1

He was elated. She was coming towards him. She was rushing down the steps. He saw her coming towards him very fast, as though she were flying, with her long bird's head, her domed forehead, her piercing eyes. When she was against him, when he felt her breath upon him, then, close as she was, he felt bold enough to move in even closer. Her two little black eyes looked up into his. The more she looked, the more radiant she became. Then he took her arm. Suddenly he rediscovered her scent, her smell, her waist. She proffered her cheek and he kissed her gently on it. He sank his face into her neck. He buried his nose in the scent of her, in her hair.

Suddenly he picked up his glass which was on the bar.

'Let's go into the courtyard.'

When they were beneath the vine on the little terrace that ran along the ramparts, he threw his arms wide, took her in his arms and hugged her to him until their bodies stopped shaking, their hearts stopped beating so frantically, their breathing eased and their lips touched. Their lips pressed together and they kissed softly.

*

She had heard nothing Simon had said to her. Her back was covered in sweat and all she had taken in was 'Let's go out to the back yard.'

At the back of the café there was a glass door full of little tinkling panes, two tables with bench seats and a little vine in a terracotta pot.

There they kissed.

She felt a drop of water on her arm.

'It's going to rain.'

'I don't think so. Sit down under the vine. There, look, you'll be under cover there.'

He had pulled the bench towards her.

She had sat down beside him. It was raining on her hand despite the big new leaves of the vine above her.

'You're wrong, Simon. It's raining.'

'Come now, Claire, those aren't rain clouds.'

When he placed his hand on the soft fabric of her cotton dress, then quite against her will she could feel her thigh begin to tremble a little again beneath his fingers, as the mild June shower enveloped them.

*

By the edge of the cliff, near a block of light grey granite that was covered in white and yellow lichen, retained the heat of the day and was still quite hot at dusk, there was a yellow bush. She immediately rediscovered the rocky nook of times past above the beach at Dinard. For, even in those days, their evening trysting place was marked by a yellow bush, on the western side of the hill, above the L'Écluse mussel beds, opposite the Pointe du Moulinet. Back then . . .

You had to go by the outer path, to climb up below the villas, slip into the shade of a gorse-bush full of thorns and little yellow bell-flowers, and sit yourself down on a long, flat, warm stone covered in yellow lichen.

You could see all the beach huts as far as the casino at Dinard.

Sometimes he joined her there in the evening.

But most often she believed he was going to join her. And that was enough for her to begin speaking to him in her heart, without let-up, as though he were there, and telling him all the events of the day.

*

'Look there, that white underbelly, that's a guillemot.'

'Where?'

'Just beneath the broom bush.'

*

She had discovered that, if she leant over, then from where this new yellow bush stood on top of the cliff—halfway between La Clarté and Saint-Énogat— she could see him leave the harbour in his motorboat between seven and eight in the evening, going past the lighthouse tower, exiting the channel, with the mooring at La Clarté on his right; he was going home to his wife, to his so-handsome, so-serious son, to their villa directly on the sea front at Saint-Lunaire.

*

She walked for whole months, for the whole of summer, in a heightened state of pleasure. She always set out from the heath. In the brown darkness of the heath and the first pale light of day, she would clamber down the rocks. And she would climb up after dinner. The light was either uncertain, golden, granular—the light of fable. Or very brown or black. Or pale but opaque. Or pale green. She moved into the Ladon farm long before the planned date, as early as 21st June, Midsummer's Day, without any great effort or trouble, without attempting to furnish it, without even wanting to repaint it, cleaning everything with Madame Andrée, just washing everything with lots of water. She loved this extremely simple place, this place without plumbing or electrical wiring, with no leaks and no power cuts, set into the rock, hidden among the hazel trees. To go down to the harbour, she would walk round the Notre-Dame chapel car park. The sea was dazzling down below. She would take the steep cliff stairway. Dazzled at first, with her eyes burning for the first fifty steps, she had to walk down in the heat and the light, but suddenly she found herself plunged into the shade of the cliff.

With the sudden darkness, she felt dizzy. She would cling on to the iron rail, never taking her fingers from it. She no longer tried to look down at the slate roofs and the little human outlines that had grown so precise below her now.

The grey houses came one by one, with all the flowers of spring on the narrow grey window sills. She barely raised her eyelids; everything was outlined sharply, standing out miraculously in the shade that engulfed the place down as far as the quayside.

When she passed the upper church, she was coming to the end. It was the antepenultimate flight of steps. Her joy increased at that point. Past the presbytery, she took the post-office steps. She went under the watchtower at the post-office corner, then under the corbelled structure above Simon Quelen's chemist's shop which adjoined it. She pushed open the door of the chemist's, Simon was waiting for her. On one of the very first evenings, almost as soon as she arrived, he closed all the lights in the dispensary and lowered the electric shutters. They went along the quay, reached the point where the boats were moored, and he showed her the long sardine boat which he fished from and used to stock up the pharmacy, and took every evening to go back home to Saint-Lunaire.

It was a 20-foot-long, single-masted craft, and he had added an outboard motor to it.

He called it his lugger.

Later on, they went fishing for sole, mullet, gurnard, little red-spotted plaice.

*

Simon showed her the whole coast from the sea.

Everything Claire had known since childhood, had known forever from the land—from the rocks and the steep paths, from the precipitous cliff stairways and the heath—she now discovered from the sea.

*

On the evening of Bastille Day, she felt obliged to go down to the harbour for the fireworks. Old Man Calève had come to take her down there in his Renault Espace. They went right over to Dinard and from there took the island shuttle, so as to arrive feeling fresh at La Clarté.

Claire Methuen didn't want to give the impression of shunning her neighbours, her new fellow citizens. The whole quayside was full of people. She danced with Old Man Calève and Évelyne's boyfriend. She danced the farandole with Fabienne and Noëlle. Mireille was there with her new husband. Claire watched the mayor inviting the town's oldest citizens to dance, one after the other. After the farandole, Simon came up to Claire.

He said, 'I'd like to introduce you to my wife and son.'

Claire said, 'I don't want you to.'

'They're going away tomorrow, for a fortnight at Gwenaëlle's parents.'

She turns her back on him. She waves to Fabienne. She climbs the two hundred and forty-eight steps alone in the warm night.

She climbs them quickly. She is sick at heart.

*

On Sunday, 15 July 2007, Simon's wife and son went off on holiday to Gwenaëlle's parents.

Simon went to fetch Claire. They went out in his lugger. Simon wanted to show Claire his villa. Sitting in the prow of the boat, Claire looked out to sea.

A bank of rocks, which the mayor of La Clarté had had brought and deposited in the sea, formed a kind of jetty.

The landing stage gave directly on to a little sloping lawn.

He came alongside it, stood up and held out his hand, but she didn't want to disembark. She didn't want to enter his house.

*

The next day, Monday, at a remote point on the coast, he again held out his hand to her. Then he knotted the rope around her waist. The cleft they were in, situated behind the wall of rock, wasn't visible. It was very dark. When you began to descend, you couldn't see the bottom.

'You go first,' shouted Simon.

Claire went down the rock face, clinging to the rope.

She put her foot on a tyre.

At the bottom of the cleft there was, first, a lot of rubbish. There was the tarred roof of a boathouse, covered with tyres, bits of rubber, plastic bags. Then came the dogwood, brambles, grass, rushes, blackberries and piles of straw. Later she came with secateurs. She opened up a kind of narrow path that eventually reached as far as the stream she was intent on beautifying.

A tiny valley ran along the bottom of the cleft as far as a creek that could only be glimpsed, but not reached because of rock falls from the cliff.

They made love there, out of sight amid the dead wood, the flotsam, the plastic, the tyres, the darkness and the rocks jutting out of the water

*

When they touched, she had discovered immediately, at the age of thirteen, that she felt an absurd sense of weakness. It was a very strange experience and, all her life, it happened only with Simon. In the past, when she was in his arms, when she could feel the hardness of his member, it was as though she was overtaken by drowsiness. Once again now, in the cleft in the rocks with him and in the little valley in his arms, she is overcome by a spreading lifelessness, akin to fainting—an extremely ancient sensation, almost older than sleep. And once again, it is as it was all those years ago. Whenever she undresses him, whenever she sees him naked, she wants to fall, her eyelids close automatically, her eyes can hardly make out what she is doing, what he is doing.

*

The sky was entirely white. They were on the beach at Dinard. She was looking around her.

Ten yards away, a bare-chested young man with a baseball cap on back-to-front and a heavily sunburned back, was sitting on a rock drinking a beer.

She lowered her eyes and looked along from the tiny dune to the white wooden fence, the path that ran beside the rocks and the spray of the waves.

She said: 'Simon, I'm happy.'

'Me too.'

They fell silent.

She touched his elbow.

'Would you like to come to my place? Right now?' she murmured.

'I don't want to do that,' he replied.

'Why?'

'For the same reason you don't want to come to my place.'

'What a pathetic answer!'

'No.'

'I think that's a really Simon answer.'

'Yes,' said Simon.

*

She formed the habit of using the rope to go down alone into the cleft in the rocks, having first taken care to fill a little white nylon backpack with something to eat, drink and smoke. She'd wait for him among the birds and the crabs.

It was a bit dangerous, a bit awkward to make the descent alone, in spite of the rope, because you had to slip between the rubbish and the rusted, broken agricultural implements. But if you didn't lose heart and got across without injuring yourself, washed your feet in the stream, stripped naked, washed yourself from head to foot and lay down in the little three-foot-wide valley that was always shaded, always cool and dark, it was paradise.

*

'Now, Simon, you're going to say, "I'll call you" and you won't call me.'

'No, Claire, I'm going to say, "I won't call you." And even if I called you, you shouldn't come.'

'God!' she says, 'the sheer quantity of nonsense I'll have heard from you!'

*

They are thirteen years old. Simon is the same age as Claire—barely two months older. He comes running out of the water between the mussel beds. It's low tide. The wind is from the north. It's a chill wind, whereas the sea is still quite warm with the heat stored up in summer. They are on the verge of their fourth year at secondary school.

She is still sitting behind her rock, sheltered by her yellow bush above the Plage de l'Écluse.

He clambers up towards her with difficulty, going through the mussel beds, clinging to the rocks.

Simon sits down a little way below her, his bottom on the black granite. She looks at him as the cold makes him shiver, though his wet body glistens. She gets up. She takes her towel. She wraps him in the towel.

'You went a long way out. I couldn't see you.'

'The water's good.'

'It looks cold.'

'The water's better than the air.'

She rubs him down. She doesn't dare to rub his soaked, black, shiny trunks with their various lumps in them. She looks at his thighs with their covering of new hair. She looks at his face. She looks at his Adam's apple, which is all angular and new. She moves aside. She lays out the towel. She smooths the folds for him to stretch out on it.

He sits down beside her.

She looks at his hand on the granite rock.

The end of each finger is wrinkled by the sea water.

She gently places the open palm of her hand on the back of his. Simon turns his head away briskly, but he doesn't pull his hand away.

He is shivering.

'Tomorrow, for the last day of the holidays, we'll go and swim together.'

He murmurs a sort of assent.

'We'll go as far out as you like,' says Claire.

Claire strokes Simon's fingers. She is thinking of the lycée. She notices his member which is now violently swelling the fabric of his swimming trunks. She takes her hand away and gets up.

'You're cold,' she says.

She is standing now.

'You should get dressed.'

'Stay,' he tells her.

But she takes his arm and pulls him to his feet.

'Come on,' she says, 'I'm tired of sitting.'

He is standing. He is sullen. He comes towards her. He snuggles up against her. He is still soaking wet. She can feel his hard member throbbing between their two bellies. He puts his mouth to her lips. They kiss. They aren't kissing for the first time, but it's the first time they've kissed at such length. She snuggles up against him. They kiss again when, suddenly, she feels his breath cut short. His breathing becomes a moaning on his lips. She stays pressed up against him for a moment. Suddenly she pulls away. He isn't looking at her. She lets go his hand.

'I'll wait for you,' she says, not looking at him.

He goes back into the sea.

*

In early July 1977, they both passed their baccalaureate. In July, Simon went off on holiday with his parents. In

August, he went to his grandparents'. They met up again at the end of September. That was after Paul's new school year had started at Pontorson. It was before university term began. Simon went off to do medicine at Caen. Claire was going to do several language degrees at Rennes. At Dinard, the coastal path is called the Promenade du Clair de Lune.

'I've been waiting two hours for you!' says Simon outside the Maison de la Cale on the Promenade du Clair de Lune.

'I was with Paul,' says Claire.

'So what?'

'I'm sorry, I was with Paul.'

'Didn't you know I was waiting?'

'I knew you were waiting but I didn't know Paul would come home today. He came back by bus. He'll be in the third year this year. My brother only comes here once a term. I wasn't going to leave him at home alone. You always forget we're totally alone now in our parents' house.'

'Because you don't want me to come to your house.'

She doesn't reply. She feels his warm hand pressing on her back. The bend in the coastal path means they are out of the wind. He pulls her towards him, close to his neck. Her lips brush against the metal of the zip of his anorak. She closes her eyes.

'I'm going to Caen tomorrow,' he says.

'Shall we write to each other?'

'Of course.'

She wrote to him from Rennes. He wrote to her from Caen. Then they stopped writing to each other. They disappeared.

CHAPTER 2

'You can't know how happy I am you've come to see me.'

Claire is standing by the table at the back of the living room. Now, when she comes, she goes to see the new films Madame Ladon has bought or the ones she has rented from the DVD shop in Saint-Malo. Some way off, in the kitchen, she hears the kettle suddenly hum then rumble. She hears the sound of the china being placed on the tray. Two little spoons tinkle. A shoe scrapes on the floor. Madame Ladon emerges. She puts the tray down on the low table in front of the sofa, leans over, pours the tea and suddenly, noiselessly, puts the teapot slowly back down on the tray and holds out the sugar bowl. Claire sits down, shakes her head, Madame

Ladon takes a cube of white sugar which she slips into her cup without touching its porcelain sides, letting it melt a little before letting go, lets herself fall into her orange armchair, leaves her ailing leg outstretched and leans forward and tugs on her skirt.

At last, she relaxes.

Then she closes her eyes.

Without opening them, Madame Ladon says: 'You can smoke if you want.'

'I can go outside to smoke.'

'Stay here.'

'Are you sure you really don't mind?'

'Not at all, I've always liked the smell. And not just the smell. I like the actions that go with it too.'

She opens her eyes.

'It's a strange dance, you know?'

She closes her eyes again.

'A very calm dance. Very beautiful. The smoke rises.'

She barely half-opens her eyes.

'Go on then, my dear, smoke,' orders the old woman softly.

Claire lights her cigarette. Then Madame Ladon says: 'I'm going to die very soon, I can feel it.'

'Madame . . .'

'Be quiet, my dear,' she replies curtly. 'I beg you. Let me speak. It's time. I'm all right. I'm at rest. Here's what's going to happen. In a month or perhaps two, I think I'll be in the retirement home beside Saint-Malo hospital. I've already reserved the room. I've already paid. The window looks out over the harbour basin. It's very near the film shop. I've got it all worked out. As soon as I'm not able to move, as soon as I'm in pain, it will all be ready.'

Claire gets up.

'You're in good shape, Madame Ladon. If you carry on talking like that, I'm warning you, I'm leaving.'

'It makes no difference whether you want to hear this or not. Whether you go off to Alaska or Peru, your ignoring it won't make any great change to my state of health,' retorts Madame Ladon.

'My God!' shouts Claire.

'And I don't see how a divinity is going to be of any use to me.'

'Can *I* help you?'

'Definitely. You can help me. In fact, you're all I have.'

'You mustn't talk to me like this, Madame Ladon, or I'm going to cry.'

'Who else have I that I love? At this moment in my life, you're the only one. That's how it is. Cry if you want. The main thing is for you to sit down, smoke your cigarette nicely and pin back your ears.'

Claire sat down. She was trying not to make any noise and holding back tears.

'Let's examine things coolly. You don't have a mother. I don't know why, but when I saw you again, one market day, on the square at Dinard, just in front of the horrible Post Office building, you came into my life as though you were my daughter. You live in a farm that belongs to me. By that I mean that it isn't yours and, if I die, everything becomes complicated for you if it turned out you wanted to stay there.'

But Claire has opened the French windows. She's already made it into the garden. It's very hot. There's no wind.

*

A tiny breath of wind may perhaps have ruffled the big blue hydrangea. But that summer the wind was like a memory. A little dust was trying to rise around her shoe, on the edge of the shoe, but it immediately subsided. The wind had made itself very scarce. When there was some wind, people said: 'Oh! There's some wind.'

People watched the branches, watched the leaves on the trees, watched the washing hanging out, watched the spiders' webs, but nothing moved. It had gone.

She went over the rocks to get back home. She clung to them with difficulty and struggled to climb over them.

As night fell, it was extremely hot.

*

She was standing in her rocky shelter with its little Dorset Heath plants, her cheek against the hot granite, against the little golden yellow lichen. It was Saturday. Though only nine in the morning, it was already very hot. With difficulty, on account of the curtain of mist making its way along the coast, she saw Simon, his wife and their little boy arrive. They climbed up on to the quayside, stooping as they went. The football the child was carrying slipped from his hands. He ran after it. Simon held him back, bent down on the quayside, got on his knees on the old cobblestones, held out his arm and grabbed the ball from the waters of the harbour.

*

It grew even hotter.

The birds stopped singing.

The hum of the insects had taken over.

As early as nine o'clock, nine thirty, she would come back home. She gave way to the tourists and the walkers. They all walked interminably, noisily, in Indian file, given how narrow the paths were. They ate everywhere. They drank everywhere. Everywhere smelt of urine.

*

The leather of the armchairs and sofas was scorching hot. She had to get up every two minutes to unstick her bare thighs from the beige seat of the Renault 4.

*

'I'll meet you at the Indian restaurant on the square,' Simon told her.

'All right.'

She switched off her mobile.

She was first to arrive.

There were tiny yellow curtains at each little window.

She was sitting in a carved armchair with her sweaty bare thighs on a fluffy pouf.

She looked at the clock-face on her mobile. The mayor of La Clarté was five minutes late.

She placed the palm of her hand on the teapot that was steaming in the torrid air. She got up.

'How much do I owe you?'

She left.

She opened the four doors of the Renault 4 before getting in.

Once again her mobile vibrated in her hand, but it wasn't Simon. It was Mme Andrée calling. Mme Ladon had had a nasty turn on account of the heat.

*

At the hospital, from the window above the Bouvet Basin at St Malo, you could see the harbour lock.

'Call me by my first name,' she said.

She tried for all she was worth. She couldn't manage it.

'I can't,' said Claire.

'Call me Mum,' Mme Ladon asked once again.

Claire was incapable of doing that.

'Call me Mum,' Mme Ladon said a third time.

'I won't be able to,' admitted Claire.

She couldn't find anything more to say. Claire took the hand hanging from the bed. She stroked Mme Ladon's fingers.

Suddenly the patient wanted a cigarette.

'Smoking's not allowed, is it?'

'No.'

'Then I want to.'

Claire looked down at the wrist, so disjointed and knobbly, the fingers so fine and intricate, and slipped a cigarette between them.

Claire's fingers struck the match.

Trembling, she held out the flame—adding to the heat—towards the glistening, deeply affecting face of the dying Mme Ladon.

CHAPTER 3

The sound of a chair being pulled across the tiled floor downstairs woke her.

Then there was a little bang from somewhere on the stairs, followed by another creaking sound quite close by.

Someone was walking around on the first floor, making the boards squeak as they did so.

The sounds she could hear were really unusual.

She opened her eyes.

She sat up on her bed. She was naked, she hadn't put a top sheet on the bed. It was so hot. Little matter, she rushed out.

She opened her bedroom door, the corridor was in darkness.

She stood stock-still.

She heard a new sound in the left-hand bedroom. On the tips of her bare toes, she moved forward. But, as she was about to go round the stairs, still by the stairwell, she saw a dark figure coming out of Paul's bedroom.

Claire stood still once more.

The figure was coming towards her without seeing her. It was a woman smaller than herself. She was wearing a dark scarf around her face. She was holding something in her hand.

Claire remained motionless.

She thought she recognized that body.

A tiny, very shapely woman, who looked strangely like Gwenaëlle Quelen, ran off down the stairs.

Claire hesitated because she was naked, but she followed her.

The door to the Ladon farm flapped open in the night. Claire couldn't manage to close it again. The lock had been forced. She opened the door wide. She looked outside. All was silence.

*

The inside of the Renault 4 was stifling. It smelt of rubber. They preferred to get out of the car and sit at the terrace of the café in Saint-Briac, above the harbour. The stalls of the fish market were empty.

Simon didn't believe a word of what Claire was telling him.

The sun was setting. The water sparkled. So much so that it burned your eyes if your gaze lingered on the wide ocean.

To the left there was a tractor pulling lobster pots across the wet sand of the beach towards the refrigerated lorry. The tide was high. It left only a thin stretch of shore. The sand was full of black pebbles. The incredible heat produced waves in the air that moved up the beach like great whitish snakes distorting the shape of things above the shoreline and the dolerite pebbles.

There was no autumn that year. The heat stayed around. Beauty lingered over the rocks. The water glittered like gold every day.

*

Madame Andrée called Claire. She explained that Mme Ladon had had to be taken to the intensive care unit at Rennes. Claire immediately got into her car and went to pray at the chapel inside the yew trees at La Haye du Routot. She did as she did when she was a little girl: the two yews at La Haye and Le Routot's tawny owl—that way, you were protected from everything. Then Mme Ladon came back to Saint-Malo.

Claire went to the hospital every day.

Every day she drove down to Dinard, took the island boat and landed at Saint-Malo. Mme Ladon was all skin and bone. Her fingers had grown quite dry. Her skin put Claire in mind of the little soft, hairy leaves of olive bushes or lavender.

*

The roses were completely flat on the ground, muddied by the storm's terrible winds, crushed by the wheels of the cars and caravans that had all left.

They slammed the two doors of the Renault 4 shut simultaneously.

They left the car park without exchanging a word.

Still without a word, they went into the new nature reserve. Beside the lake were cast-iron benches painted blue.

They walked over to them.

All the ducks came out of the reeds, came up to them, spoke to them. They were asking for food. But Claire and Simon had nothing on them.

The ducks and drakes regarded them with sudden contempt. Realized they wouldn't be throwing them anything. Went off again in silence.

Then Claire and Simon together, standing face-to-face, Claire taller than Simon, clasped hands and the four hands rose in the air. They talked, gestured, fell silent.

They lowered their arms.

They sat down on the wet bench. They watched the water falling on the water.

*

On Sunday, 28th October 2007, the clocks went back. Sunday, 28th October was the day Claire and Andrée brought Mme Ladon home to St Énogat, at 10 a.m. Sunday, 28th October was the saint's day of people called Simon or Jude.

When Mme Ladon got home, when she was back in the familiar warmth and smell of her own home, the painful expression on her face faded and life was easier.

Mme Andrée placed a Tupperware container on the low table. 'I found sea spaghetti at the market. I've put some pasta on to heat up. You just need to put them in the microwave.'

'What is it that you call sea spaghetti, Andrée?'

'I don't know what else to call it.'

Mme Ladon leans over, her hands are trembling. She manages to get the lid off the Tupperware container.

'Oh, those. At Toulon we called them *truilles*.'

'You'll see, they're very good in pasta.'

'I'm sure they are. Andrée, you're a treasure.'

*

'On the 28th of October, every year, the evening of Saint Simon's day,' explains Mme Andrée, 'when everyone got home, we used to eat the first chestnuts, boiled in milk. We crushed them with a fork. It was pretty unpleasant. The next day, at dawn, at the hour when the embers were being poked and the fire re-lit with cardboard packaging or bits of old crates picked up in the market, we put them by the logs. And once the chestnuts were roasted, we went to the church, to the churchyard, and placed them on the family tomb.

*

'At last, she's gone!'

Mme Ladon gets up from the sofa with the help of her stick. She is as thin as a rake. She goes into the corridor, cautiously pointing the end of her stick in front of her. She points to the double door with it.

'Claire, come and see. Look. Could you do a bit of painting for me?'

Claire comes over. She sees where the paint has flaked off.

'Of course.'

Mme Ladon comes back slowly from the kitchen, dragging her left leg. She is carrying a sprig of little cherry tomatoes in a hors d'oeuvres dish.

Claire walks round her. On the low table she lays out the tray, the glasses, the chilled Chablis.

'Are you in pain?'

'This leg won't move at all these days.'

She sits down gently. She leans her leg on the magazine rack. They raise and clink their glasses.

Claire reaches over the little dish of cherry tomatoes to Mme Ladon.

Mme Ladon bites into a little tomato and gently half-closes her eyes as though the taste were exquisite.

Then she keeps her eyes closed.

She begins to speak, her eyes still closed.

'Listen, my dear, I'd like to ask you a favour. It's been bothering me for some time. Are you listening?' asks Mme Ladon very quietly.

'Yes.'

'How would you like to be my daughter?'

Mme Ladon suddenly raises her eyelids and stares straight at Claire.

'I'm alone,' says Mme Ladon. 'You're alone.'

'I have my brother.'

'I've got brothers too. They've passed on, but I didn't love them.'

'I love Paul.'

'As you say. Though I don't really see the connection. I've no intention of leaving my house to my nephews or to anyone from my husband's family. I inherited it from my father and how it is now is down to me. By the way, did you go and see the farm up on the cliff top?'

'But I've been living there for at least four months! Mme Ladon, don't you remember?'

'I'm happy to hear that. And how is it?'

'It's very good, Mme Ladon. I've told you. It's very simple, very plain, very clean. With Mme Andrée's help, it's been cleaned from top to bottom. The main house is very cool. Whereas the sun's been so hot here all summer, it's been in the shade and wonderfully cool. We emptied it, washed it out and did it up over a week. That was with Mme Andrée before the summer—don't you remember?'

'Of course I remember. My leg hurts too much for me to go there with you. There's so much to do.'

'Yes.'

'Claire, I've known you since you were really little.'

'Yes.'

'Let me talk a bit, will you?'

'Yes.'

'You worked hard on your Czerny and your Hanon, you started on your "best-loved classics" when you were orphaned.'

'Yes.'

'Your aunt died when we were at Fauré's *Barcarolles*.'

'Exactly.'

'You see, my memory's still intact.'

'Yes.'

'In short, you're really alone and I'm really old. You understand what I'm saying. We'll sign some documents, the two of us.'

Claire has stood up. She is saying nothing. The proposal seems horrendous. She doesn't know why she finds this sudden kinship so terrifying. She's incapable of thanking Mme Ladon for the offer made to her.

*

On the jetty, the woman from Rennes's six girls are roller-skating. With furrowed brows, curled lips and billowing skirts, they skate along at great speed and in great silence, one after the other.

Claire stays hours watching the girls dashing around, dancing, manoeuvring, swaying, turning back on themselves, breaking from the pack, until their mother screams to them to come back up, have their tea and do their homework.

*

She goes as close as possible, bowed under the force of the wind, her head forward and her hair white and stiff falling over her eyes, on the cliff edge.

It is cold.

Now the sun was far off in the sky.

Now the colours of fabrics were extraordinarily varied. Now you could see without being blinded or dazzled. Sometimes reality returned. Sometimes night extended itself gradually into the days. Sometimes the tarmac was solid and painful to fall on. Sometimes you could forget the happiness of summer. Sometimes you had to struggle against the wind again and protect yourself from the cold.

*

It was the day after All Saints'.

She was walking in the mist, between the sand, sludge, seaweed, pebbles and seashells.

Dawn was approaching, the dew was returning.

Now, with the dawn, there was a sort of hail landing on the stones.

The path seemed as if it were made of crystal.

She was coming back from seeing Simon. She was filled with wonder at the beauty of the path across the heath.

*

It's evening. She can see the smoke rising from the hazel wood, straight ahead, in the middle of the heath.

She likes how it looks.

The long black trail of smoke suddenly sinks beneath the force of the wind, blown off towards the setting sun.

She stops the car suddenly on the path.

She runs.

In front of her, the little wood surrounding the Ladon farm was on fire.

In the middle of the little wood, the main building was burning down.

The firemen were there and the people from the thalassotherapy centre. There was a huge crowd of onlookers standing around, mostly helpless.

PART THREE

Paul

CHAPTER 1

From the age of three to the age of thirty, I had six nervous breakdowns. As these collapses were getting more frequent and longer-lasting, more distressing and disabling, I went into psychoanalysis. After eight years of it, once I'd just about emerged from the depths of hell and become more or less a living being, there was no one waiting for me back in the daylight. I was even more alone, but much less anxiety-ridden. I was almost free. Suddenly, all the anxieties, all the forms of paralysis I'd suffered up to that point were dispelled, shattered. They were all overcome together. Then I was standing on relatively solid, relatively frozen ground, bathed in a fine light, its transparency become, as it were, external and infinite. My brain was thinking in flexible, varied, quick, surprising ways. I was still afraid, but I wasn't afraid of my fear. I could even draw strength from it. I could even contemplate the world for its own sake; enjoy the cold; enjoy going out when it was pouring down; enjoy the low clouds, the sense of abandonment, loneliness; love walking aimlessly in the dark. What an extraordinary shore the world presents when it has suddenly become immense, intrusive, incomprehensible and totally indifferent to oneself! Then it's like birth. And what a pleasure not to be assailed, with each recurring dawn, by panic anxiety about the day ahead! One day near the clinic where I'd managed to get myself six months' rest—where I'd learnt to get back a few hours of sleep—I'd gone as far as a little river that wound round on the edge of the grounds, near the fence beside the road. It was so far away and the weather was so cold that no one was brave enough to go there. So I went several times, posted myself there, knelt down on the dead leaves and the moss and shouted down the river, shouted louder and louder, shouted as loud as I could, downstream in the freezing air. Then, when I realized I was perhaps traumatizing the snails and frogs, I suddenly stopped. In any case, I had very few people to shout to any more in this world. I didn't have a mother any more, I didn't have a father. I had no regular friends. I lived alone. I was earning a lot of money as a cereals broker. And the burden of transporting the raw materials that occupied my days didn't fall on me: all

I carried around were little mobile phones, a small portable computer and some flash drives. The whole lot fitted into a small rubberized bag that took up little room in my case. That was my whole office. My whole office fitted into a wheeled suitcase that was my constant companion. I worked at home, or at the clinic, or at the hotel, at the homes of companions or people I knew—anywhere. I was scrupulously attentive to Stock Exchange hours and changes in the market. I found plenty to fill my spells of insomnia. I was rather asocial. Music affected me deeply. It was the only thing that could ease my sadness and bring distraction from the sediments of the day and their memory. At least I'd found nothing else that so consoled me for the little excess of loneliness that had worked its way inside me. I listened to music several hours a day. Now one day, or more precisely one evening, when I was already fast asleep (I have no regular times for sleeping), the telephone rang and woke me suddenly. It was my sister Marie-Claire calling. She was a translator. She spoke at least fifteen languages, whereas I spoke only six. She was in tears, which really wasn't at all usual. More than that, she was calling for help. I was reluctant at first, then I realized by the sound of her voice that something odd was going on. I got out of bed and dressed. I got into my car, drove across Paris and went to bring her the help she was wanting from me. It didn't occur to me for a second, as I found her leaning against a tree in the rain on the corner of the rue de Lübeck and the rue Boissière in Paris, opposite the Guimet Museum, that my life was dramatically changing course and that I was saved.

*

My sister was as long, tall and fair as I was short and dark. As well as being very tall, she was very thin. Mum was tall like her but she had dark hair like mine. Mum was Greek. She hadn't had much education but she had the same gift for languages as Marie-Claire, or Claire, or Clara, or Chara. I don't know how many names Marie-Claire had given herself over the years, not being satisfied with her own. There was a whole string of them; there must have been some sense to it but I never grasped it. I never tried to. Chara is very common in Greek. It means grace, but she was no more a Greek than I was a Bushman. Long and tall, not really graceful, very serious, stooping, she looked like a bird of prey. Even as she aged, she remained as thin as a reed. An old reed. Only Claire's hands deteriorated with age. They thickened. They grew red from gardening, from messing around in seawater or rock pools, from clinging to granite rocks.

As for her voice, it got higher as she got older. Higher and higher. Her lips grew thinner and thinner. Her nose too got thinner. Her soft blonde hair became mingled with big coarser white locks—very white.

She dragged me off to our childhood village, which until then I'd shunned like the plague.

There was always a very peculiar suddenness and intensity to her life. She didn't so much take decisions as find herself overrun by bursts of energy; driven along or halted or devastated by them. In those moments, the blood drained from her cheeks. The corners of her mouth quivered. I asked her: 'What's going on?'

'Nothing', she replied systematically.

And then she looked over at a man crossing the street and going into a chemist's, a man called Simon Quelen. He was her childhood friend. He was a chemist in a tiny, prosperous seaside village.

I said: 'You're still looking at him.'

'There's no way you can understand.'

This man, who loved fishing, outdoor pastimes and the little town where each new election saw him returned as mayor, had become her obsession. There's no other way of putting it. Actually, I couldn't at all understand what she might be feeling, since I'd never been in love. I'd never loved anyone. I'd not even the faintest idea what that might have been like, never having been confronted with anything that could have borne that name.

*

And so in 2007 at forty-six years of age, just before she reached forty-seven, Claire stopped travelling all over the world and translating in Shanghai, Stockholm and London. She sold the very stylish little house she owned in Versailles. She got more money for it than she needed to live on. It has to be said that her new style of life in Brittany required extremely little money. She spent her time walking. She was always outdoors. Not a book. Not a record. Not a newspaper. Not a magazine. No red meat, nor fancy foods. Hardly any clothes. A lot of Camels, unfiltered Chesterfields, Peter Stuyvesants, Rothmans Blue, lots of wine, vegetables, olive oil; a wholegrain or spelt loaf every two or three days, since she couldn't bear her belly to be podgy or round. Fruit on market day. Not much fish—which she bought for a song at the harbour café. Essentially crab, prawns, cuttlefish. Her biggest budget item was tobacco. Hence the only thing she asked me to bring back from my travels were cartons of mild foreign cigarettes. The more foreign, strange, unknown, unpredictable, disgusting, improbable and incomprehensible they were, the more she liked it.

That was what my sister was like.

The older she got, the less I understood her.

The more she lived outdoors, in the open air, looking out over the sea, the easier she was to get along with.

I knew immediately when my sister was anxious. She suddenly became sweaty. Her long skeletal body streamed with sweat. Her eyes widened. You could read her like a book.

Her mind, when she was anxious, had something a little drunken about it.

If her eyes suddenly sparkled, that meant she was thinking of something to do with Simon.

When her only thoughts were of Simon, she was radiant.

She thought about him so much that she was never alone.

*

When we were small, my sister and I, we really saw very little of each other. We met up for a month once a year, in August for the long holidays, at my uncle's farm. It was the only time of year we were together. She spent much more time with Simon than with me. At Easter, I stayed at boarding school. We stayed alone, a fellow pupil and I, in the empty boarding school, secretly touching each other, secretly smoking, consoling each other for our loneliness, daydreaming, doing lots of work, hoping for another life. Michel and I were very successful in our studies later on. In summer, in the month of August only, Marie-Claire and I were inseparable (Simon had two months of summer holiday, a month with his mother and father and another with his grandfather and grandmother). Of course my sister was older than I was. She tormented me. She mocked me. She told me off. She taught me things. She gave me a hard time. For the whole of the month, she humiliated me because I was much less talented than she was. She looked down on me for being much smaller, but, all the same, we were together twenty-four hours a day. For an orphan, nothing's more important than being accepted by someone else, whatever they do. Whatever I might say or do, she defended me. Never mind that you could cut the atmosphere with a knife at Pont Touraude and how nasty our cousins were to us. We slept side by side in her big brass bed in her room. Her bedroom didn't smell good at all (the musty clothes, the mould on the floor, the toilet bucket, our big shoes). A little river—a beck—ran across the farm and into the lock. We splashed about in it, far across the fields, in the rather sparse shade of the fruit trees, as soon as it got very hot. Brittany is very hot in summer. We bathed in the lock. She taught me to swim. We went to the beach (a sort of mud beach adjacent to the estuary) by slipping under barbed wire and crossing two fields, despite our Uncle Armel having forbidden us to cross that neighbour's land. There was a camp site. Then you came to la Grève des Marais. It was there, at the end of the day, that Chara taught me what little Greek I know. It was our mother's language. Our uncle's main concern was to see as little of us as possible. He avoided me whenever I appeared. His own children were much older than Marie-Claire and me. We were left to our own devices until dinner time. We went to the market on our own, with two francs each, money Aunt Marguerite took from what the wardship arrangements granted her and handed over to us. As soon as Auntie 'Guite died, Simon's parents took over as our guardians. So, during the week, Claire not only went to the lycée with Simon but lived with him in the evenings, sleeping above the chemist's shop at Saint-Énogat, in a separate bedroom. Then the Saint-Énogat local authority took over our wardship and we finally came back home.

I mean by this that my sister was never 'in love with' Simon Quelen.

You can't even say that she had 'feelings' for Simon Quelen.

In her whole life I don't think she put her arms around him more than a few times, but she loved him for more than sixty years. It was an unconditional bond. She spied on him every day in the last years of his life. She watched him each day until his terrible death. She was a spectator at that death—and was even, I believe, terribly happy that it occurred.

At different times she felt bursts of violent, unexpected, hugely powerful irritation towards this little boy—then this adolescent, then this man—and they left her in something like a state of desolation.

I believe that was the most enigmatic thing about her, and the most terrible. When it happened, she became completely motionless. She sank into an incredible state of dejection. She was like a piece of flotsam, washed up on a totally unknown shore.

At times she cursed herself for having deliberately forsworn the rare pleasures that would have been afforded her by the man to whom she was so indissolubly attached.

She stayed whole days, whole nights behind her bush, spying on him, quite motionless.

She saw him walk on the beach, pull out his dinghy, go into the sea, start up his motor or hoist his sail on the sea when he took his lugger out; she saw him casting his line, fishing with a dipping net or a cast net.

At the merest hint of dawn, the hope of seeing him led her down to scan rocks, sea and shore for a glimpse of his silhouette among them.

CHAPTER 2

I remember it was Fabienne Les Beaussais (the Dinard postwoman) who called me. Not only had Claire disappeared, but the farmhouse she was living at in Brittany had been set on fire. I immediately called my cousins at Pont Touraude, who had taken over the farm by the river Rance: they knew nothing about anything. In the end, I caught a plane. There's a little Ryanair airport at Pleurtuit (a stone's throw from the Methuen farm). But it was Fabienne who came to pick me up and went to see the gendarmes at Dinard. They were at a loss. They had questioned her. They'd seen what a state she was in. They could understand our anxiety. They didn't see what they could do. Then Fabienne had the idea of asking Mme Ladon. She was in hospital. We had to go to Saint-Malo to see her. Fabienne and I went into her room. I asked her where my sister was. She was very weak. She couldn't remotely understand what I was asking. But as soon as I mentioned Claire's name, she opened her eyes.

'Where's my daughter?'

'No, not your daughter, Mme Ladon. I'm talking about my sister. Do you know where she is?'

She didn't have much breath left but she called Simon Quelen. At least I held my little mobile near her mouth and she did the talking. The mayor of La Clarté told us to come over. He thought he knew where he could find her.

We crossed the Rance again. We went straight to Saint-Lunaire. There, led by Simon, we walked back in the opposite direction along the sea front. We followed the cliff edge. We had to get across a dump with rubbish up to our waists, then, after an old battered caravan, we crept under some big rolls of barbed wire that had fallen from the top of the cliff, under a tarred shed roof, some driftwood and piles of straw.

We arrived at last on a tiny bare slippery path, covered in moss and mud. It was a winding, steeply sloping path and it led to a tiny valley where we found her sleeping on some tyres.

Simon went off immediately with Fabienne.

He didn't want to approach her.

He said he was going to fetch the emergency services.

Claire was suffering from hypothermia. They wrapped her in shiny blankets. She was immediately taken off by the first responders into one of the nearby treatment rooms at Dinard thalassotherapy centre. The doctor examined her, prescribed lots of medicines, an antidepressant, a sleeping pill.

Marie-Claire went back to sleep.

An hour later she was being taken by ambulance to Mme Ladon's house at Saint-Énogat, to be looked after by Mme Andrée, the cleaning woman.

*

With the aid of Old Man Calève and the gendarmes, I was able to establish quite quickly what had happened on the evening of the fire. For a time my sister had stood transfixed by the ruins of the main building. The hazel wood had burned, but the rest of the farm wasn't really damaged. The firemen had left. Using a little motorized pump, they had taken water from the pond and put the fire out. Some of the bricks still had a halo of steam above them, which Claire, unwilling to accept anyone's help, was left to contemplate alone.

She was reluctant to go back to her car as people tried to persuade her to (she had abandoned it on the heath when she had seen the smoke).

She was just standing there helpless, not knowing what to do, outside the wreckage of her farm.

The neighbouring farmer, Calève, suggested she have dinner at his house and spend the night there.

She declined.

'You're going to catch cold, Mme Methuen,' he said. 'I'll call your cousin Philippe.'

'No, absolutely not that, Monsieur Calève' she mumbled. 'I won't have that.'

And she shot him a fierce glance.

She was sitting on the iron bedstead—it had been thrown from the first floor onto the earth of the farm-yard.

In front of her, before her very eyes, the cast-iron shell of the cooker was smoking.

The big armchair was completely burned.

In the garden, the corner of the orchard hadn't been touched by the flames. The whole of the eastern corner, the cowshed and the pigsty had been spared.

A gendarme had told her: 'The fire must have started very early this morning in the kitchen.'

She stopped him. 'That can't be so. I left for the hospital at Saint-Malo at nine. When I left the farm, everything was normal.'

'Then it must have happened just after. It's the farmer from the Ferme du Roc, just above the thalasso-therapy centre, who called the fire brigade.'

'Old Man Calève?'

'Yes, he saw the smoke and called the firemen. The people from the thalasso centre got here just after that. Everyone was very helpful.'

The farmer (Old Man Calève) confirmed this.

'At noon the fire was terrible. The firemen got here at one but it was too late. It was like a furnace. I thought a gas bottle had exploded.'

'I don't have any gas bottles,' said Claire. 'Apart from the wood-burning stove, I just have an electric hob.'

They'd put very light, interlocking tin fencing round the main farmhouse. When night had fallen completely, she had left.

Later, she admitted to me that she'd seen Simon, looking pallid, and he'd beckoned to her. He'd parked a hired lorry up by the Pierres Couchées, just at the point where the path met the car park. The door was open and she'd gone over to him.

'It was my wife.'

'What?'

'I think it was my wife.'

'Are you sure?'

'No, I'm not sure.'

'Then perhaps it wasn't her.'

'She hasn't been in a normal state since yesterday. She's . . .'

'Simon?'

'Yes.'

'What if you stopped thinking about your wife all the time?'

'I don't have any evidence. I've no evidence, but Gwenaëlle's acting very strange.'

'So turn her in. Dump her at last. Let's run away together—ten thousand miles from here. Wherever you want. Where you go, I'll go, Simon.'

'No, I won't leave my son in the lurch—not in the state he's in. No, I won't abandon my wife. There's no way I'm going to leave them, but I'm going to help you. I'll help you. I'll pay what it's going to cost you, but I won't turn her in. Even if I had evidence, I wouldn't do it, Claire. I don't want to. It's our fault.'

'That's completely stupid. Our loving each other hasn't made your wife an arsonist.'

'Yes, it has.'

'Stop it.'

'She's the mother of my son.'

'Stop it. You don't realize what you're saying. Who am I to you if I'm not your wife, if I'm not the mother of your son?'

*

The next day a gendarme had called her on her mobile and asked her to go to the police station as a matter of urgency.

She had slept in her car.

She went to the police station right away.

'It wasn't an accident, Madame.'

She clutched hold of the door.

'Go on.'

'Take a seat, Madame.'

'No need, go on.'

'There was a petrol can in the kitchen.'

'In the kitchen?'

'Do you have riding boots?'

'No.'

'It's a woman with riding boots who burned your house down.'

'It isn't my house, it's Mme Ladon's.'

'Does Mme Ladon have riding boots?'

Then Claire had started laughing. She was suddenly crying tears of laughter. She explained why to the two gendarmes and they began to laugh along with her as they imagined an old woman with a zimmer frame walking out of Saint-Malo hospital in riding boots to set fire to her own heathland house with a can of petrol.

*

She'd gone back to the heath.

Suddenly, she told me, she'd seen a hired lorry arrive, going at full tilt and honking its horn madly on the path that led to the Pierres Couchées car park. Simon was at the wheel. She carefully parked up her Renault 4 on the verge. He braked violently when he reached her. He shouted out: 'We have to talk. Let's meet at Dinard. At the Balafon at twelve.'

He drove off.

*

They had lunch.

With his elbows on the table, he had leaned towards her. With his mouth in her hair, he had murmured in her ear.

'I don't want to see you again.'

She didn't reply. She was, I imagine, pained beyond words.

'We must never see each other again.'

'I'm not deaf.'

They said nothing for quite some time.

Then she had said she loved him.

'I love you too,' he said, 'yet I shan't come to see you again, Claire.'

'I've got it, Simon.'

He squeezes her fingers. He grips her fingers. He suddenly wrests himself away. She sees his back. He's pushing open the café door. He's walking into the wind. He doesn't turn round. He walks on. He goes down past the tents in the marketplace. Someone calls out to him and he doesn't reply.

Claire runs off. She hides. She goes back to the little valley in the cleft in the rocks, to the edge of the tiny river that's just a stream. No one finds her. No one knows where she is. Fabienne calls me, etc. That's probably more or less how things went.

*

Yet Simon and Claire saw each other one more time, one last time. After she'd been found, after she'd been examined, treated and knocked out with sleeping pills by the doctor at the thalassotherapy centre, Claire moved into Mme Ladon's house with Mme André at Saint-Énogat. She still wasn't sleeping at night; Mme Andrée would go home and, with Mme Ladon still in hospital, Claire would take advantage to carry on her wanderings along the coast, as she pleased, until morning. One morning, having come down as far as Dinard harbour by the Promenade du Clair de Lune—it must have been six a.m.—she decided to go back home through the town.

She rushed down the hill at full tilt. The wind was blowing at her back. It was pushing her and she was almost running, carried along by it. The wind blew along the dead leaves on the pavement. It was pushing them towards the market place. She wanted to pass by the little Balafon restaurant on Dinard marketplace where they had seen each other for the last time.

She quickened her step when she saw the same hire lorry.

He opened the door to let her in. He kissed her hair, her cheeks and her hand and drove off.

They drove across the town. They were heading for the other side of the bay. They crossed the Rance and went as far as Cancale, where they had breakfast. They talked about the insurance. He thanked her for saying nothing. There would be no investigation. He signed the cheques.

'From the very first day, Claire, we kissed in front of everyone. We shouldn't have done that . . .'

'It's too late, Simon.'

'We should have been cautious from the off.'

'Tell me why I should have been cautious.'

'Well, at least I should have been.'

'You? How could anyone be more cautious than you?'

Claire took the cheques from the table.

'I'll drive you home.'

'I'd rather get the bus.'

'*Adieu.*'

'*Adieu.*'

A slim figure wearing a white shirt. Over her skirt a little brown duffle-coat floated unbuttoned. Her blond hair was wet. The hire lorry receded across the fields.

CHAPTER 3

Each morning, as Claire was getting back into shape again, taking her drugs, sleeping, talking to her psychiatrist, I walked the streets of the town, went up by the cliff route and gradually found my bearings again in a world where I too had lived as a child. I clambered about the mussel beds, the piles of seaweed and the rocks, as I had when I was ten or eleven. I tried all the cliff stairways one by one. One day I went up a little stairway with wooden steps, where only the winding path had been dug out of the granite. I slipped under the barbed wire. I walked across the field of oats. Through the broom and across the heathland. I ended up walking along the rue de l'Anse-au-Genêt. To my great surprise, I found myself in the middle of Saint-Énogat, the only person walking around the little town. Some extraordinarily precise sensations came back to me. At last I got to the square where the church stood. The garden round the church was full of giant hydrangeas. There were still some winter roses. I recognized the place at once and the church as well. I couldn't resist the desire to go in. I went up the stairs and pushed against the leather door. It resisted. I put my shoulder to it and pushed again but at that point I realized the church door was closed.

I left the shade of the porch and went and sat down on a bench in the garden. It was three strips of varnished wood swollen by rainwater, lost among the giant hydrangeas. I closed my eyes. I could smell the tremendous fragrance of the air—the rock samphire, the rotting hydrangea at the foot of it, the cold, soaked boxwood plants. I suddenly caught a smell of dark tobacco. I opened my eyes. A man of about forty in a black turtleneck was standing there. He was holding large keys and also had a cigarette between his fingers.

'Did you want to go into this church?'

I nodded.

Laughing, the priest raised the keys he held in the tips of his fingers, which were mingled with the smoke from his cigarette. He clinked them against one another. He went ahead of me. It was like a ceremony. He threw his cigarette into a bush. He went towards the porch and I followed.

'I'm Father Jean,' he told me.

'Paul's the name.'

'All very nicely religious . . .' he mumbled.

'You needn't have put yourself out.'

'It's no trouble. I came to visit an ageing colleague but he isn't in.'

'You have the keys.'

'We all have a complicated set around these parts. We're always standing in for each other on the coast. There are so few of us now.'

The church was very dark. The leather door closed quietly behind us. All the noises of Saint-Énogat's main square faded away.

In the half-darkness, the first thing I saw was a table that was blocking the way in the middle of the central aisle. It was covered with dark-red prayer books. Jean walked round it and up to the choir.

I stayed there in the dark, at the back of the church, standing by the table with the prayer books, by the heavy humidity of the font.

I could see Jean, who had knelt down at the altar.

He had powerful shoulders.

He had put his hands together.

I walked up the aisle without making a noise.

I sat down on a straw-bottomed chair precisely in the second row in the choir, on the right, third seat along. That was my place when I was a little boy. We went to mass at Le Minihic-sur-Rance. That was where the big church was. My sister Marie-Claire was on the other side of the aisle with the women, next to Aunt Marguerite, on the left.

Then I too closed my eyes in the silence.

After a while we left the church. He held out his hand to me. Behind us was the newsagent's postcard stand.

'I served at Mass here,' I told him.

'You're from Dinard?'

'I was born here, at Saint-Énogat. I was a boarder at Pontorson. In fact, I mainly served at Mass when I was at boarding school.

Jean put his hand on my arm.

'At Pontorson? So you were an orphan?'

I nodded.

'I live in the next little port,' said Father Jean. 'I was an orphan too.'

I was suddenly very moved. I said nothing.

'Surely you know Saint-Briac?' he asked.

'I don't think so.'

The name meant nothing to me.

'It's the next village. I have to go there now. Come and eat with me.'

'I don't want to put you out.'

'You're not putting me out. I don't like eating alone and I spend my life doing it. I've been eating alone for two years. Help me out!'

I called Claire on her mobile.

'Things OK?'

'OK.'

'I'm going for a bit of a wander.'

'Right.'

'I'll be with you for dinner.'

'All right.'

We came to the harbour. We waited for the shuttle boat that served Saint-Énogat, l'Anse-au-Genêt, Plage-Blanche, La Clarté, Saint-Lunaire and Saint-Briac. The next day was Armistice Day.

*

The second time I saw him was the following Saturday. I arrived before evening Mass. He hadn't seen me. He was standing by the sacristy door. His hands were clasped over his stole. He was getting ready for the confessional. Two parishioners were waiting. He was very handsome, with the stole and its fringes over his black woollen pullover. The rain was beating on the sacristy window above him. His raised forehead shone beneath the naked lightbulb. There was a gold crucifix by his hand. Smoke rose along the length of the bare body of the god. The remnants of a last cigarette before entering the nave.

*

'Let's meet at the presbytery for dinner.'

'Yes.'

I met up with him at the Saint-Briac presbytery at the end of the day.

I'd brought a bottle of Corbières rosé that I got from the supermarket in Saint-Briac.

We drank in silence, I put my glass down on the table, I took his hand, he put his glass down in his turn, we fondled each other in the lamplight.

*

Claire was teasing me.

Claire said: 'You don't see it, do you, Paul? You don't just look at this priest of yours, you're in thrall to him. Can't you see yourself? You're second-guessing him all the time. You acquiesce in all the stupid things he says, go along with them all.'

'Maybe I do. Why shouldn't I?'

'You're waiting for him.'

'So you're telling me that, Claire? And what do you do with Simon? He says goodbye and what does my sister do? She waits for him.'

She shrugged her shoulders, furious.

I repeated: 'You too Claire, you look at your little mobile that you keep switched on by your bedside.'

'That's for Mme Ladon.'

'And now she's lying! You wait for him, Claire and that's normal. Perhaps that's what love is—waiting.'

'Not at all.'

'Watching the whole time.'

'That has nothing at all to do with it. Not only am I not waiting for him, but I've dismissed him from my life. Whereas you've just become dependent on a completely moronic cult leader.'

'He's a believer, but he isn't a moron.'

'You need him.'

'Yes, I need him.'

'You jump up when your phone rings.'

'Yes, I love him.'

'Are you going to leave,' she suddenly shouted.

I nodded. As I continued to nod my head, she said very softly, shrugging her shoulders and heading for the door: 'Do as you like.'

'I certainly will.'

*

It was snowing.

Little flakes that didn't stay on the ground.

'Come over to the presbytery,' said Jean.

'All right.'

'There's no more wine.'

'Don't worry. I'll do some shopping. We'll have dinner at the presbytery.'

He'd had a key cut for me. I would get there first, light the lamps, turn the central heating on and get the meal ready. I can't hide the fact that I like to cook. And I had more success with Jean than with Claire.

*

For 24 December 2007, Jean got some musicians to come to the church at La Clarté. Amiens agreed to come. But not a lot of people turned out for the concerts Jean organized, apart from a few music lovers from Saint-Malo and the chef from the restaurant at Cancale.

Jean built a crib out of wood and cardboard that was magnificent.

I put heaters all around the building: we got it up to 13 degrees.

Amiens played works by Bach, Hidden and Unsuk Chin. It was very beautiful.

'This all seems too difficult,' I said.

'Never mind. God loves it.'

'There were seven of us.'

'Music is an art we've sacrificed.'

'Seven out of a hundred and fifty residents. That's hopeless.'

'Seven in the depths of winter. That's not hopeless, it's substantial.'

'Perhaps I should have put some little posters up.'

'The mayor of La Clarté has passed a by-law to ban our posters.'

'Our posters?'

'Not ours in particular, but posters in general.'

'Simon Quelen?'

'Yes.'

'Why? On what grounds did he pass the by-law?'

'He prefers granite to music. It's more beautiful. What he said exactly was that it's more dignified. Nothing on the walls. He doesn't want supermarket adverts up there any more. This is a Green mayor we're dealing with.'

*

In early 2008, I left for the Seine Saint-Denis department, where Jean had been appointed curé and allotted a magnificent rectory in the Mansart style. Eight empty rooms, twenty feet high.

*

The caretaker of the flats in the rue des Arènes in Paris was hosing down the courtyard. She was holding the hosepipe in both hands, shooting great streams of water on to the paving stones, the dustbins and the base of the walls. I was waiting for Jean in the courtyard. It was the first time he came to the flat. I was waiting. Or rather I was doing all I could to avoid being splashed by the caretaker. I remember the joy I felt when I saw him arrive, when I felt the curé of Saint-Briac beside me, dressed in mufti, and pushed open the glass door of the lift for him.

CHAPTER 4

That lasted four months. Then it stopped. Then I came back. It was Maundy Thursday 2008 when I came back. Two days later it was Easter. Claire was still living in Mme Ladon's house at Dinard. The farm wasn't habitable yet. Claire had told me she'd bought the ruined farm from Mme Ladon. But she'd given no thought to the building work, so I rolled my sleeves up and threw myself, with great pleasure, into the minor 're-building' of the main farm building. Thanks to Simon Quelen, we got connected to the water and electricity supplies. I was able to install some modern conveniences throughout the farm. I made a bathroom downstairs and a separate toilet. I had heating put in. I lowered the ceilings of the bedrooms to make the attic habitable. At noon each day, I went to have lunch either at Saint-Lunaire, a rural landscape predominantly yellow, or at Plage-Blanche which, despite the name, was more grey and pink or, alternatively, at Saint-Briac, austere and sublime (though Jean had left). Spring was mild and dull. The surface of the sea had no sparkle to it, but glimmered under grey skies. The waves were all chalky and flaccid. I went home by boat. There was no swell. In the evening, I climbed the stairway to the Pierres Couchées. The horizon was white, a marvellous, chalky, floury white, like powdered sugar. It was a mind-boggling view. I was able to see why, in an earlier age, people had put up their three enormous stones there.

The clouds in the distance were massive, too, and as slow-moving as the waves were sluggish.

One day, positioned as I was by chance on the stairway, tired from the climb, I saw my sister squatting on her rock, half-hidden by the bush.

In her cliff hideaway, she was a mere tiny dot above a great block of black granite.

She had nothing of the living creature about her, except the movement of her head and the fact you could glimpse her yellow hair among the little yellow clumps of spring blossom on the bush.

I watched her as she spied on Simon.

I was stunned by the noise made by the sea. I suddenly saw her head emerge from among the yellow buds and lean over towards the rolling white waves that crashed limply onto the brown shore. They say that brown doesn't exist in the solar spectrum. Nor white perhaps. She was doubtless in another world.

*

Even in a car, the road up to the clifftops is extremely steep. It was full of dangerous bends. It was dawn. Claire and I were going to Saint-Malo. I'd been showing her round the building site. I don't know precisely what was on her mind. Claire was driving. And now she wanted to get to Mme Ladon's bedside. In the end, the road, which had until then been tarmacked, suddenly became a path of whitish gravel. You had to be in first gear. It was still raining, a spring rain, a fast, white rain. Claire left the path, drove a little way into the grass, then cut the engine. She opened her door. Then we heard the roar of the sea in all its violence.

'It was here, Paul,' she said. 'Do you remember?'

She pointed to the guardrail and gave me a searching stare. I didn't understand what she was saying. I didn't remember.

It was, as ever, no use asking questions. Since nothing I asked her ever got a direct answer, everything stayed vague. There were no connections to anything.

That was how she lived.

It was all about stopping places, halts, sudden standstills, flat rocks, bushes, corners of walls, of chapels, of porches.

She hid beneath the porch at the corner of the harbour, waiting for the lights to go out in the chemist's shop.

I caught her like that more than once at La Clarté at night time.

Going to the lawyer's. Going to the doctor's. Going to vote for the mayor of La Clarté. Going for a blood test. As soon as there were appointments for a set time and the date and the hour were near, she was just an irritable blob of fear.

One day I caught her naked on Mme Ladon's scales. If she'd put on a pound or a few ounces at dinner the day before, she went into a foul mood, even though her legs were the long thin legs of a flamingo and her bottom had disappeared.

*

She came back bathed in sweat when she hadn't seen him from one of her hiding places. The sweat ran down her face and neck. She would towel herself down. To no avail. She would wipe her little chest. Her underwear was soaking. I ran her a bath in the brand-new bathroom. She had only to slip into the water. But, when she came out of the bath, after she had towelled down, she was streaming with sweat again. It had been like that her whole life. As soon as the anxiety attack approached, her back streamed with fear.

She was so hungry that the whole of her head trembled.

'Calm down,' I told her.

She spilt some of the soup on the table.

'Drink it slowly,' I would say. 'No one's going to take the table away.'

*

When I was a child, what particularly impressed me about my sister—she was five years older than I was—was her concentration. Suddenly, she wouldn't be listening at all. She'd be completely switched off from this world. When we were small, I'd realize this immediately. I could tell that she wasn't listening to anyone any more. It's been like that her whole life. When this was happening, her little eyes narrowed and weren't black any more but yellow, like brass, like buttercups. Her back would bend. She'd sink into an inner world where she no longer followed things with her eyes. Her gaze would harden. It would turn mischievous, fierce, glowing, sparkling. By contrast, when her pupils softened, when they went back to their ebony colour, to the colour of the rocks at Cézembre, she'd be returning to this world. She'd be watching something that had a life outside herself. Her calm in those moments was disconcerting but kindly. She was a very complex woman. There was a kind of slowness in all her movements. At any rate, there was always a sort of slowness in the answers she gave. She'd think long and hard, unhurriedly, then suddenly she'd unfold her long heron's legs. She'd get up, totter slightly, and only with difficulty take flight. But then, abruptly, she'd be off into the reeds and suddenly beyond the trees and up into the clouds.

*

By contrast, when we were teenagers, when she was humiliated by our poverty, by our aloneness and by the wealth of the Quelens, my sister wouldn't make a noise or complain or lament with either words or tears. She'd suddenly squat down, wrap her arms round her knees and bury her head in her skirt. And she could stay like that, huddled up with her forehead on the flesh of her arms for hours on end, like a rock—as dense as a granite rock—dreaming or, rather, watching her life going on in the depths of herself. She had always been convinced that she wouldn't marry him.

*

Darkness no longer afforded her cover. The days were getting longer. In the evening, she'd stay on an ever-higher step of one of the stairways leading down to the harbour. She'd observe Simon lowering the shutters of the chemist's. She'd follow him from a distance. The stairways of La Clarté lend themselves well to watching figures down below at whatever height they may be, depending on the shade cast by the walls, and at whatever height you may be, depending on the light. Simon would go to the town hall. He'd come back out with the town councillors (including Mireille and Jean-Yves) to have a drink with them on the harbour. Or he'd go down to the harbour alone and take his sardine boat out. He'd also bought a small motor boat. She'd watch him go back home to Saint-Lunaire or sail towards Dinard.

She'd follow him with her eyes or take the island boat if it happened to be in. Or the Saint-Malo shuttle for the pleasure of passing by his motorboat for a moment without him seeing her.

*

As long as he was alive, she suffered. I'd never have believed someone could suffer as continuously and as long. Once he was dead, she was happy. Miraculously, if I can put it that way, the suffering went when the presence of her beloved's body did. At any rate, her suffering stopped when it turned into mourning. It was almost wonderful to see her sad, merely sad, after so many years of pain. The body is incredibly solid. She seemed happy to be still in love with him even after death.

They no longer saw each other in the sense of meeting, speaking or touching, kissing or embracing. But they observed each other from a distance. She no longer hid so as to try and catch sight of him in the corner of the chemist's display or opposite his windows, waiting for the lights in the office or the stock room to go out. Nor sitting on the corniche looking down on the windows of the house at Saint-Lunaire to which he returned every evening, directly by sea, by the new motor boat. Once he had gone back to being faithful and a good father, good husband, good mayor and good pharmacist, Simon had begun doing a lot of sailing, a lot of fishing, a lot of sea trips. He'd repainted the hull of the old sardine boat. Every morning he came in by sea to open up the chemist's, then he went to Saint-Malo where the previous day's order was delivered. Every evening, he left again by the harbour channel. But he watched Claire too, watched her from the sea as she walked among the rocks. He too watched her wandering round observing him. He too followed her with his eyes hour after hour, the whole day. And in the same way, *she* looked down and saw him on the sea, missing her, pretending to fish, circling around, looking up at her, thinking of her, loving her and wanting nothing to do with her.

CHAPTER 5

Around the end of May or the beginning of June 2008, when we were able to go back into the Ladon farm, Claire was very agitated. She didn't like the smell of new paint and was constantly getting away from the rebuilt farmhouse—too rebuilt perhaps for her taste. In fact, she was worried about what Gwenaëlle might get up to. She was torn, again, between freedom, the wind, the cold and nature on the one hand, and, on the other, the protective but agonizing, imprisoning, suddenly scary warmth of a house I had probably made too comfortable—and perhaps too personal. In the evening that anxiety turned to agitation. I realized that, at that point, she couldn't be alone, not because she might have been frightened, but because she didn't know what to do with herself, if I can put it that way—whether to go wandering or to rest. She lacked a transitional space. I went to find Fabienne Les Beaussais, but she said no, she didn't want to take her on. She had her family and she'd have been uncomfortable taking in a woman of forty-eight (it was Fabienne who was forty-eight, my sister was only forty-seven) in that rather peculiar state, seeing as her children were still very young. It would be setting them a bad example for their future lives. I shrugged my shoulders. I decided to stay a little bit longer. I made myself a proper office in the attic where I could concentrate fully on my brokerage calls. With the electrician from Dinard, we put in more plug and aerial sockets and dormer windows. It became a fine wooden tunnel which I lined with bookshelves, TV screens and speakers. I liked it there. I had two new Velux windows installed, making the place light and airy. I was living in the sky. Claire calmed down, or my presence calmed her. She gave in more to what I decided for her, became calmer in her reactions. Sometimes she hung around a little downstairs in the morning before going off into the countryside. She washed her hair and dressed and wore her hair more or less the way I liked. She cleaned herself up systematically when she came in each evening, so as to please me. She even did a bit of cooking (eggs she'd gone and chosen from Père Calève's place, the farm at La Tremblaie) when she was alone. In the beginning I forced her to go to the restaurant with me, but in public she was really anxious, needlessly anxious. She felt uneasy with other people's eyes on her. Above all, the closed windows of restaurants filled her with horror. She felt like she was suffocating. Dreadful restaurant music upset her too.

*

She took my hand.

'Paul, goodbye.'

'Goodbye, my darling.'

'I have to leave.'

'I know, my darling, I know.'

I didn't know what to think. Once again, I didn't understand what she was trying to say to me.

'Even if he'd got a divorce,' she said, 'it would have made no difference. He'd be living with me but thinking of them. He'd be worried about the disability of the one and he'd blame me for the pain of the other. He wouldn't be with me. He'd be less with me than I now am alongside him.'

She reassured herself as best as she could. We walked over towards the jetty. I bought the newspaper. She bought cigarettes.

We sat on the decking of a café terrace and drank a coffee. It was a bit too cool to stay long. She was looking out to sea, but he wasn't there. We walked off along the sea wall. She began to cry silently. I put my arm round her shoulders. She pushed it away. She leaned against the low cement wall. I could see the tiny port behind her, a trawler coming in, in front of the renovated tower, before the lighthouse.

*

'Paul, do you remember when you were feeling so low, before you started with your shrink. You said those who don't face up to their pain are destined to suffer it endlessly.'

'Did I say that?'

'Certainly.'

'I must have read the phrase in a magazine.'

'Do you really not remember?'

'I may perhaps have said it.'

'Well, I'm telling you, it's completely stupid. First, those who don't face up to their pain suffer it endlessly. Second, those who do face up to it suffer it endlessly.'

*

Just about every night, Claire woke at three a.m. She got up in silence. She had tears in her eyes at that point. She wondered what she was going to do and if she wasn't going to kill herself. In the bathroom, naked as the day she was born, she would waver, tempted by the drugs the doctor had prescribed for her. She had to choose. Either she was going to turn the day into a soporific daze or she was going to walk outside in the terrible clear-sightedness of anxiety, accepting the occasional jolts of a so-to-speak alien force rising from time to time from the depths of the body to invade its whole space. Most often, she gave in to the emptiness, to the mysterious sweating. She'd slip on a T-shirt and go and run along beside the waves. Or she'd swim. She'd run back home and run herself a scalding hot bath.

'Mum didn't love me,' she'd tell me.

'She didn't love me either,' I said to reassure her.

'Mum was very beautiful. But Mum didn't like any of us. She hated children.'

'Do you think so?'

'And I'll tell you, she was right to hate us.'

*

Mme Ladon recovered her health. She'd been in hospital almost a year. She called for Claire. She made it clear on the telephone that she didn't want me to come. Claire became evasive and drove alone to Saint-Malo in the Renault 4. She sometimes went to fetch her and take her out in the car. She moved back into her house at Saint-Énogat at the beginning of the summer holidays in 2008, in early July, so that she could have her friend over to stay. In September, Mme Andrée brought a bottle of ouzo out on to the garden table at Saint-Énogat, a bowl of ice cubes, some pistachios in a blue bowl and some bulky adoption forms. Mme Ladon couldn't walk now, but she seemed happy to be able to enjoy her garden and lie out in an electric wheelchair that folded out as required. She was looking at the red grapes on her vine when she had a stroke. She was taken back to hospital. She never came back to Saint-Énogat.

*

I have to confess that when, after Mme Ladon's funeral, I learnt of her having adopted my big sister like that, I wasn't just humiliated but transfixed with jealousy.

It was as though I'd stopped being her brother.

We no longer had the same mother.

It was as though she were betraying me eternally.

She could at least have let me know before the children of the step-family and the Ladon nephews.

*

I remember that when Claire had gone to live with Mme Ladon at Saint-Énogat, before she discovered the heath and the farm, I'd been happy to take back the flat in the rue des Arènes just for myself. For some weeks I'd even 'coveted' the solitude I was going to get back when my sister would at last leave my place. But to my great surprise, when she'd left for Brittany, there were many evenings when, coming home, I thought my sister was still there. I thought I was going to open the door and see her towering above me. I had the fleeting impression someone was waiting for me. I was already joyful at the thought of taking the lift and reaching the landing. Barely had I opened the door and, seeing all the rooms unlit, I was disappointed, though I couldn't explain why.

And so it wasn't the joy of being alone that flooded in when my freedom was at last restored.

It was condensed silence that descended on my shoulders.

And now, for a mother, my sister had another woman than our dead mother.

It was very difficult to grasp.

Worse: it had already happened.

And now it was continuing.

My sister had lied when she'd told me she'd bought the burned-down farm on the heath from Mme Ladon.

I remember my sister sitting next to Aunt 'Guite at Mass, each with their barege shawl on their head.

When I was a little boy in church, Marie-Claire had an armchair with her name on it. I was full of envy at that. It was a beautiful, velvet-coloured armchair. Beside the prie-dieu that bore the name of Marguerite Methuen, Aunt 'Guite had had a little armchair placed for her to sit on. Every Sunday, my sister sat on the right of Auntie 'Guite in her purple armchair, whereas, on the very rare weekends that I had leave from boarding school and was allowed to accompany them to Le Minihic and the big church, I had to sit all alone on the other side of the aisle among the men, where I had neither an armchair nor any sort of wooden chair with my name on a little copper plate screwed to the wood.

My great-aunt cared only for my sister.

My great-aunt was very sensitive to the cold. She often wore a little fur tippet on her shoulders. It buttoned under her chin, around her neck. When she went to church, she slipped this little 'palatine', as she called it, under her 'raincoat' and over her 'cardigan'.

In the living room, when she was sewing, you couldn't see her head. You could only see the 'palatine' leaning forward in the light cast by the bamboo standard lamp.

*

'I'll kill you if you call me Marie-Claire again.'

'It's your name.'

'Stop winding me up.'

'Chara was completely fake.'

'It was real. Mum called me Chara.'

'She isn't even your mother any more. You sold her for a mess of potage!'

Claire looked at me horrified. She began to cry.

'A piano teacher meant more to you than Mum!'

That was the only time in my life I was so angry that I shouted at my sister. I remember it was winter. The gloomy winter of 2008. There was already a crisis in the markets. I'd sold off my main positions. I'd steered my main clients to those rare colleagues who hadn't taken off up the Amazon or gone to Vietnam. I was even thinking of selling my flat in Paris. Everything was hanging on a decision from Jean, and he'd written me a letter so 'Catholic' that I was unable to make out what it was trying to tell me.

*

Then there was a freezing afternoon in January (2009). Jean came to spend a week at Saint-Briac for New Year. He agreed to see me again, to have me over to the presbytery.

I pushed open the farm door. The cold of the heath stung my face. I went out into the freezing cold. The sky was overcast. There was no wind. The clouds above the clifftops weren't moving. Among them was a little one so very dense and black that it shone. It seemed to me I had to follow it. It seemed almost lost among the heavier clouds. And it was so intensely black that it appeared to shine, to sparkle, to call out, so dull was the rest of the sky. The grass was scrunchy, frozen, close-cropped and scorched white, as I went towards Jean's place along the clifftops.

In the presbytery at Saint-Briac, beneath the old buckled window, the monk Malo and the monk Festivus were both there, leaning down over the ship's rail, casting the net to catch the dragon of the island of Cézembre.

In the middle of the wall, the black boat of Saint Malo himself.

Beneath the boat, I grasped his hands without hesitation.

Jean wavered, then agreed to surrender his hands to mine.

He had a little more of a stoop than before. He didn't ever wear a cassock any more, just a black crew-neck pullover, black jeans, and white or grey trainers. His fingers were yellow with nicotine. He seemed a little cold. He seemed ageless. But he was more sensual than you might have suspected just by seeing him. What was called the presbytery at Saint-Briac was just two rooms on the ground floor to the left of the church. You went in through the kitchen: there was just a table, a gas ring, a stool against the wall and a wine rack, in which he put his empty bottles. Then there was a living room with a fine bookcase that dated from the nineteenth century, three tapestried armchairs and two big windows looking out over the old graveyard. At the end was a bedroom that looked out on to the courtyard and the dustbin shelter. He chain smoked. The old Breton women in the street who kissed his ring were placing their lips on nicotine-stained fingers.

Above his head, increasingly shrouded in smoke, I can still see the old painting in which Saint Malo in his boat, accompanied by his friend, was leaning down forever over the dragon of Cézembre.

And beneath the old painting in the presbytery, I can see Jean's thin, smooth face, his large forehead perpetually shrouded in smoke, his serious, blue eyes and his hollow clean-shaven cheeks. Jean had the face of a saint. He walked bent forward and quickly—with the furtive quickness of an old man. His hands skimmed over handrails without pressing on them. He walked genuinely very fast.

When the complaint was lodged by the parish, Jean was called to see the bishop. I went with him to the bishop's palace. Jean went ahead of me, moving quickly over the black and white paving. He had a distinct stoop that day. We went up a staircase and walked through dormitories full of young priests or students or seminarians and an interminable library. At last, Jean opened some big double doors. We found ourselves in a particularly austere dining room. Large paintings, sooted and not easy to make out, hung from the walls. The table was laid for three. We remained standing, glass of wine in hand, waiting for the bishop. I have wonderful memories of that lunch. The bishop asked us not to attract so much attention to ourselves. At the end of the meal, he blessed us.

PART FOUR

Juliette

CHAPTER 1

The snow is melting at her feet.

The young woman is leaning forward a little, her long auburn hair gathered in an absurd big brown pony tail, dripping with melted snow. She is very tall. She is taller than Claire herself.

'Can I sleep here?'

'Who are you?'

'Your daughter. My name's Juliette.'

Dumbfounded, Claire opens the door.

She lets her daughter in, lets her go through the kitchen, unzip her jacket and take a seat in the living room.

*

'How did you get our address?' asks Claire.

'You can call me "young lady" if you prefer, Mum. To answer your question, let me point out you're both in the phone book.'

Juliette has sat down in the blue armchair.

'You don't like me calling you Mum?' she asks, lifting her head in Claire's direction.

She doesn't answer the young woman.

'Perhaps you have someone in your life? I'm disturbing you. Are you ashamed of me?'

'I don't have anyone. It's Paul, your Uncle Paul, who lives here with me.'

'Am I an inconvenience?'

'I don't know.'

'Are you ashamed?'

'No, I'm sure of that. I'm not ashamed.'

'You're not ashamed, but I'm an inconvenience.'

'Well, yes, you are an inconvenience.'

*

Claire followed the big pony tail as it climbed the stairs.

'That's my room,' announced Claire.

'Can I sleep here?' Juliette asked her mother, eyeing the adjoining room.

'If you like.'

'Who normally sleeps there?'

'My little brother slept there. But he's moved into the loft now.'

'Uncle Paul?'

'Yes.'

'I've never seen him.'

'No.'

'Who havc I known actually?'

'No one.'

'Did I know you?'

'No.'

'I'm going to put my things in there.'

'As you like.'

'Do you have a towel so that I can dry my hair?'

'Follow me. I'll show you where the bathroom is.'

*

It's six in the morning. Claire comes into the kitchen. She goes straight to Juliette's little radio/alarm-clock and switches it off.

'No radio,' she says.

Juliette gets up from the table without saying a word. She opens the kitchen door and goes out on to the heath.

*

Claire has joined her daughter on the heath. The snow has melted almost everywhere. You just had to avoid the slushy paths. You had to walk on the sodden grass and heather instead.

The fog was yellow.

The masseuse from the thalassotherapy centre came running by.

Suddenly, the young athlete stopped. Bending down, she picked up some dead wood and made it into little bundles on the path. She put them in her backpack and took them for lighting her fire in the evening.

Above her, the snow still clinging to the branches glistened gently.

'What do you want, Juliette?'

'Take me out for a meal and I'll tell you.'

'I don't like restaurants.'

'Take me to a café then.'

'When are you leaving?'

'When I want to. Then I'll say, "Mum, I'm leaving." But, you see, I lived with a woman who didn't even say, "My darling little daughter, my little Juliette, forgive me, I'm leaving".'

*

'How's your elder sister? How's Marguerite?'

'She has seven children.'

'Is she happy?'

'Her husband's taken over Dad's business.'

'Are things going well?'

'She didn't want me to come.'

'But are things going well for her, for them?'

Very softly, Juliette told her: 'If you really wanted to know how things were, Mum, you should have stayed.'

They were standing by the wild roaring sea.

*

Juliette has brought back a gull. She is tending to it on the kitchen table.

'Do you know your way around gulls?'

'A little bit.'

'Are you a vet?'

'No.'

'What then?'

'A natural-science teacher.'

Claire looks at her daughter.

'You handle it very delicately.'

'It's a magnificent blue-backed gull.'

'Are you going to feed it?'

'Yes. Since you're not doing anything, Mum, go fetch whatever you can find now the snow has melted. Worms by the pond. Slugs. Snails. Anything.'

*

'In the end, we both went to the restaurant,' said Juliette. 'Suddenly I saw the tongs—the tongs for breaking crab shells—that Mum was holding start to shudder all on their own.

'Then she put them down gently on the tablecloth.

'She got up suddenly, sobbing. I didn't know what to do. I didn't understand. It wasn't my mother I was seeing but a little girl running away, heading full tilt for the restaurant door, leaving in a flash, disappearing. It really was a habit of hers, running away. It came as second nature. Then, without daring to look up, I felt all the eyes from all the other tables in Saint-Énogat's restaurant converge on me. Everyone had fallen silent. Everyone was looking at me. When I turned round I saw a man (I'm told it was the mayor), his son and his wife who were having lunch together, sitting around a large dish of seafood.'

*

Juliette goes back to the farm.

'Mum, I don't love you.'

'Yes, my girl.'

'It makes me feel good to say that, Mum.'

'Yes, my girl.'

'Ciao.'

'Goodbye for ever.'

CHAPTER 2

One day in early autumn 2009 (it was Thursday 1 October), Mme Andrée called Claire. She explained that Mme Ladon had had a stroke. They were both in the clinic at Saint-Malo.

'Claire, can I hand you over to Mme Ladon?'

'Are you in the room?'

'I was in the corridor. I'm going through. Right, I'm in the room now. I'll put her on.'

Claire heard a voice that sounded very weak.

'My darling . . .'

'Yes,' said Claire.

'I'd like you to come over.'

And Mme Ladon began to cry.

*

'Hello, Mme Ladon.'

The room smelt of disinfectant, flowers, old age, rubber, face powder.

Claire held out the little box from the cake shop.

'I've brought you some macaroons from Saint-Énogat.'

'From which baker's?'

'The one by the church.'

'Good for you. That's the best by a long chalk. What flavour?'

'Pistachio and raspberry.'

'You remembered. You're a charming child. You spoil me. Ah, I'm being spoilt!'

She was hampered by the tubes in her nostrils. Not only did her voice not sound as it usually did because of the little tubes, but curiously it had lost its normal tone. Her torso was propped limply against the pillow and she couldn't move her head. Claire had to sit on the bed, grasp Mme Ladon's hands, look her directly in the face and pronounce her words with exaggerated lip movements to make herself understood.

When Mme Ladon answered, her jowls began to tremble as she was speaking.

'I'm being spoilt!'

She repeated: 'I'm being spoilt! Look, I'm like Louis XIV. I've got a chair on wheels and I'm drinking Burgundy!'

*

'I didn't want children. I really didn't. I never regretted that.'

She began to sob again. 'I think I should have.'

'Well, to some extent you have me, Mme Ladon.'

'No, you're not my child.'

Claire suddenly fell silent. She shrank deep into her plastic armchair.

Mme Ladon went on: 'I had so many children to occupy me with the music lessons—singing, theory and piano! But I was wrong, do you see? I should have had a child. What strange bodies we have! What strange ages, such uncoordinated ages our bodies impose on us!'

*

Claire Methuen can see Mme Ladon sitting in her wheelchair in the dining room to the right of Reception. She's eating. She's at the 'wheelchair table'. A care-worker is holding the spoon and helping her to eat from time to time. Claire prefers to wait. She's standing behind the screen, beside the counter at Reception, waiting for the meal to be over.

'Will you push me as far as the goldfish pond?' Mme Ladon asks Claire Methuen.

The old woman is pale. Her face has lost its expression. The left half of her mouth is paralysed. Her hand is a cold bird's claw on the end of a bone.

Claire pushes her across the pink paving stones of the courtyard.

'A bit further.'

She looks at the goldfish.

She looks at the fountain.

'It seems strange to me to still be living in this world.'

Claire's hair is longer than it was. It's all white and stiff at the front. It falls over her eyes and hides her tears.

*

When Claire Methuen came back, Mme Ladon wasn't breathing.

The young woman pulled up the plastic chair, brought it to the head of the bed. She sat down right beside Mme Ladon's corpse and leaned over.

She put out her hand.

She took the cold hand, the hand so light, in her palm.

She stroked the bones that were so fine beneath the skin of her hand.

She stroked the skin, so gentle and flaky as it is with dead people, like the thinnest of pancakes.

She stroked the slim, dead fingers one by one.

*

'Hello, is that you, Paul?'

'Yes.'

'It's Claire.'

'Yes.'

'Claire, your sister.'

'I know. I recognized your voice. What is it? Is something wrong?'

'Yes, it's not good. Do you remember Mme Ladon?'

'Yes.'

'Well, that's it.'

'That's what?'

Claire doesn't answer.

'Has she died?' asks Paul.

'Yes.'

'Are you alone with her?'

'I am.'

'Do you want me to come?'

'Perhaps.'

*

At Mme Ladon's funeral, in the church, on the back row on the right, at the end of the pew, Claire is standing, unseen, wearing a headscarf she has borrowed from Mme Ladon. Right at the end of the row. Her pain is plain for all to see. It's Father Jean, Paul Methuen's friend, saying

Mass. Mme Ladon's stepchildren and nephews stand side by side in the front row.

*

'At Mme Ladon's funeral,' says Paul, 'the weather was awful. Beside the open grave, Jean simply pronounced these words from the Gospel: "God said: *Salvum facere quod perierat*. I came to save the lost." Rain was falling on his face. There was no let-up all day in the torrential rain. Jean walked round Mme Ladon's stepchildren and nephews and handed Claire the basket of sodden roses first. She behaved impeccably. She did all she should. She took a rose from the basket and threw it into the open grave. Then she too walked round Mme Ladon's stepchildren and nephews and presented the basket of roses to Mme Andrée. When my turn came, I gave the sopping wet basket of roses to Jean, I took Claire by the hand, brought her under my umbrella and we left.

'No one—neither I nor the others—knew as yet that Claire was her adopted daughter.

'No one, except Mme Andrée suspected she was going to inherit almost everything the old piano teacher had to her name.

'Claire took the wheel. As the Renault 4 was struggling up the path, there was a fall of snow. Rain then snow, and everything started to slide around. We parked as best we could at the Pierres Couchées car park and ran across the heath to get into the warm.'

*

'A few days later, Claire told me she was inheriting almost all of Mme Ladon's possessions. We were coming back up from the mini-market. I couldn't grasp why.

"Marie-Claire," I asked.

"Yes."

"I'd like to get a handle on this."

"On what?"

"I'm afraid it sounds like a bit of a fantasy. Why would your old piano teacher leave everything to her pupil?"

"She loved me."

"But how come you inherit everything? The family will take you to court."

"No way. I'm her daughter."

"You aren't her daughter."

"She adopted me."

"She adopted you?"

Stunned, I fell silent. It was more than I could cope with. The pain felt terrible.

"Who is this Mme Ladon who's suddenly burst on the scene, adopted you and made you her heir, even though you never mentioned her in over forty years?"

"You were at Pontorson. I was under Aunt 'Guite's thumb at uncle's farm, pestered by the uncle and plagued by the cousins. The wardship was interrupted when Aunt

'Guite died. I found myself on my own in our parents' home at Saint-Énogat. In the afternoon, after school, I went to the Quelens'. In the evening I was alone. My social life has never been more intense. After the Quelens, one old lady after another invited me to dinner. All Aunt 'Guite's friends took up the baton so I'd never be left to my own devices. I was a queen (she cried when she spoke of being a queen), they gave me little tarts to eat, and pancakes of all kinds, choux pastries, waffles, oublie biscuits, macaroons, craquelins. Nothing was too good for me. Mme Ladon, my piano teacher, made fritters. That was on Thursdays. We made them together. I always shaped them to the initial letters of our parents' names. I made Ps and Ls too."

She shot me a strange look.

I said: "L for Ladon?"

She hesitated.

"If you like. I was the one who threw them into the boiling oil. While I was doing that, Mme Ladon made her speciality—Neapolitan *zeppole*. It was my piano teacher who taught me to draw. It was my piano teacher who taught me to sew. She had the most beautiful hands in the world. She had long, fine, nimble hands, fast, virtuosic, extraordinary hands. She was small and yet her hands were highly articulated, genuinely more articulated than ours. She was a great performer on the piano. I always looked forward to the moment when she would 'show' me the new piece."

Tears were streaming down her face.

"Take the wheel."

"We're parked, Claire."

She got out of the car.

The sea, intense in its blackness, gave off barely a glimmer. The winter sun shrouded everything in a bright, grey, smooth, magical mist.

She looked out to sea.

A surfer in his black neoprene suit, sheltered by his grey wave, was sliding along in silence off the rocky headland.

I left her to stare at her surfer.

I took the wheel of the Renault 4 and set off to Saint-Briac to get back to Jean.

After the downpour, a sort of mist was trying to rise, drab as the sky, at the end of the esplanade at Saint-Briac.

The terrace at Saint-Briac's restaurant, a structure built on piles, stood directly above the beach. That was where I met up with Jean. He was leaning against the railing, smoking a cigarette.'

*

'I'm seeing him again. I go every Sunday to hear him preach.'

'Where?'

'In one of the parishes.'

'I'm ashamed of you!' Claire exclaimed. 'I'm ashamed of my little brother!'

But in the end she was happy that her brother was happy.

Jean gave a very fine sermon on St James's words: 'Your riches are corrupted, and your garments are moth-eaten. Your gold and silver is cankered . . .'

Then, after that sermon, Jean moved into the farm.

*

Claire is standing in front of the big Breton wardrobe in Mme Ladon's bedroom. She passes a pile of cardigans to Fabienne Les Beaussais, who stuffs them into a brand-new leather travel bag.

Claire empties the two glass shelves in the bathroom.

'What are you going to keep?' Fabienne asks her.

'I'm going to keep the whole of the corner with the papyrus plants downstairs. Perhaps it'll be to my liking one day. She loved that corner. It was the corner where the piano she taught at used to be. If the piano had still been there, I'd have kept the piano.'

'I wouldn't have minded the films and the DVD player myself.'

'Take them.'

'Oh no. You watched them with Mme Ladon.'

'I did that to please her. Personally, I'd rather be out walking. All images bore me. Take them.'

'No.'

'Take them, I tell you. I don't know why I so much prefer seeing things live. I think I'd go so far as to say I detest the images of things.'

'What about Mme Andrée?'

'She's already taken all she wanted and she'll have the money we're going to get from the rest. We've discussed this. Do you know, I don't think I actually ever went to the cinema—not once in my life—for the pleasure of it. When I was thirteen or when I was twenty, I went for the kissing. But that wasn't a pleasure in images. Deep down, everything about cinema seems fake to me. It seems to me all the people in films act very, very badly. It's distressing. The fakery upsets me.'

'In that case, my dear, I'll take them.'

*

The coach doors open simultaneously. It is a pilgrimage. The little girls, encased in their uniforms, hands clasped and feigning prayer, file awkwardly into the cemetery.

Claire pulls back.

A group of nuns follows them in.

'How beautiful!' say the little girls, standing by the gloomy graves.

Claire begins by moving away from Mme Ladon's tomb. Then she tells herself, 'The children are right. The trees are beautiful.'

Then she sits down on a grave. She watches the little girls pass by in single file. She looks up at the branches above them. Suddenly she gets up. She reaches out to the branches. She shakes one. She shakes down the old fruits and the seeds. She pulls her handkerchief from her jacket, unfolds it and puts the seeds in. She'll take them back to Mme Ladon's, to the garden at Saint-Énogat. She'll put them in the ground when she gets back. When spring returns, they'll germinate.

Then she plants some secretly on the heath. That's how she develops a passion for flowers and bushes and the whole heath becomes her garden. All her country walks grow around her. 'I'll go this way, I'll go that way. I'll think of this spot, I'll think of that one. I'll possess a little of the beauty of this spot, I'll have a little of the beauty of that one too.' All these beauties will be alive. All beautiful things live. She said to herself: 'Living things are always memories. We are all living memories of things that were beautiful. Life is the most touching memory of the time that produced this world.'

CHAPTER 3

Through the whole of spring, the bad weather flung itself at the heath and the cliffs. It brought with it darkness, torrential rain and the lowest, blackest clouds.

No one put out to sea.

No one ventured on to the stairways or terraces.

For Claire, 2009 passed like a bad dream.

*

'The recession swept my job away,' said Paul, 'and I fell in love with this little farm my sister had inherited from her old piano teacher. I did all I could to weatherproof it. I planted bamboo and willow, both to soak up the water and to replace the hazel trees that burned. The bamboos crowded out the willows. I created a kitchen garden where I mixed in flowers with sage, thyme and gooseberry bushes. Claire didn't want to see the flowers cut. She got rid of the vases. I bought a hot cooking stone. I added an extension to the garden table and grilled squid on it. Or scallops. I sautéed them for just a second—just long enough for them to cry out and die—on the burning stone.

Claire said: 'Aunt 'Guite used to use an iron hook to lift the hotplates on the range that was fired by wood or coal. She cooked meat like this too, directly on these circular hotplates.'

I said: 'Aunt 'Guite was an idiot. I didn't like her. You were the only one she liked. She wouldn't let me do anything.'

'What are we eating tonight?'

'Cockle soup.'

'Aunt 'Guite used the dialect word *rigadelles* for clams.'

'And a panful of lightly toasted blackberries.'

'That's happiness,' said Claire.

'At last a serious comment from my sister.'

*

There was a cowshed by the pond. I had it knocked down so I could enjoy the sight of the sprawling bamboo grove on its own.

Claire let out the house Mme Ladon had owned at Saint-Énogat.

When she was here, she wasn't afraid any more. She liked to walk in the night. She felt safe as soon as she was plunged in darkness. She liked to feel the fresh night air on her face, to feel it seep into her clothes, ruffle her hair; she liked to be completely enwrapped by night, near to her sweetheart, near to the idea of her sweetheart, enwrapped in the sound of the sea, the tang of the sea.

*

Paul opened the waffle-maker. Claire said: 'You bastard, how much weight will we put on with that? Half a stone?'

He was delicately buttering the inside of the mould.

'What are you making?'

'A *far breton* with prunes.'

'A stone, then.'

'So what, that's what you weigh now,' muttered Paul.

Claire said: 'You don't understand. I want to look good for him on the beach.'

'You're a skeleton. A white ghost on the beach.'

'That's how he likes me.'

'White?'

'No, ghostlike.'

*

One evening Paul catches her skulking in the entrance beside the chemist's, her hood down over her eyes. The whole hood is covered in snow.

'What are you doing here?'

Claire huddles close to him.

'You're here again?'

'Shut up!'

She's anxious. She gestures with her chin towards the windows that have a light in them.

'So what?' asks Paul.

'Those are his windows.'

'He lives at Saint-Lunaire.'

'Not always.'

'Come on.'

He grabs her arm.

'Come on.'

She breaks free.

'Leave me, Paul.'

She pushes him away.

'Go away.'

Paul goes off, furious.

*

'The finest thing in winter,' said Claire, 'is the sun. It's what Mme Ladon called sunbursts. Walking in sunbursts—even freezing winter ones—beneath a clear, empty sky, letting the pure, harsh air into your lungs.'

When it's sunny, he brings his boat out.

Watching him in the bright sunlight.

*

One day the leaves from the trees that had suddenly been stripped bare were all in a heap on the sand. Blown along by each gust of wind, they piled up in the creek at the bottom of the concrete stairway that led up to the pillbox. Then they disappeared.

*

On 24 December 2009, Juliette came by. She looked tired.

'Because of you, I went to see Marguerite. Everyone's well. They're still as rich and there's still as many of them. There's no problem, the children are working hard . . .'

'You're not exactly crazy about them.'

'No, I don't see them much. You know, Dad's dead.'

'So I assumed.'

'Why did you assume that?'

'Otherwise, you wouldn't be here.'

She takes her in her arms.

The next day, she takes her back to Saint-Malo by the island boat.

Because of the different stops it has to make, the crossing takes almost an hour. It's raining. Juliette is cold. She goes back inside the boat.

But Claire gets anxious when she's inside. She stays out on deck, her face in the salty air, the wet air, amid the noise of the gulls that screech as they circle around. She puts her brown hood up. In the distance she can see La Clarté. She looks at the coast and the white sea crashing against it. She contemplates all her various journeys from the reverse angle—the paths, the stairs, the creeks, the birds and their nests.

*

Easter 2010 and she was outside on the square at Saint-Énogat. She was watching him through the restaurant window.

Simon came out of the restaurant.

She was just in front of him, by the newsagents, her hand against the trunk of the oak tree. He went up to her. She put out her hand and gently took his arm. He made to speak to her, but changed his mind and plunged his face into her hair, into the crook of her neck, and squeezed her to him.

Then Simon went off without a word, walked away. He went past the Jules Verne fountain and down to the beach.

*

When the first sunny days arrived, Paul planted a lawn running from the fishermen's path in the north to the shell of the old Citroen lorry. He had the farmer from La Tremblaie come over and tip a cartload of new soil on to the kitchen garden and show him how to revive the orchard, which wasn't thriving. Working together, the two of them managed to dig over the ground. Old Man Calève taught him how to prune and layer the branches of the trees. The birds came back when the fruit did. Claire adored the kitchen garden. She tended it every morning. She grew yellow tomatoes, chervil and parsley. She asked Paul to put a tap on the outside of the house. A long yellow hosepipe ran to the tomatoes. Old Man Calève took charge of training the pear trees against the wall of the orchard, a wall that protected it from the storms that came off the sea fifty yards away, on the edge of the cliff that fell sheer to the bay.

*

One morning she opened the door. It was summer.

She crouched down in the sun near the little windmill palm.

She watched him in his boat, crossing the bay.

*

She was watching him from the top of the rock.

He crossed the lower end of Saint-Énogat beach where he had left the white boat belonging to the chemist's shop. He pushed the boat out, grasped hold of it and started the engine. It sped off on the waves, jumping from one to another a bit like a boat with an outboard motor.

She ducked back into the shadow of the rock wall as best she could. She was hidden there by the mass of granite, but she watched him leaning out.

He was fishing.

Later, he pulled on the chain and raised the anchor, his gaze riveted on the black mud that swirled around the anchor in the dark waters.

She looked up.

There were sunflowers all along the plateau that led to the cliff, to the West. Every evening there was a marvellous hedge of them, a golden boundary marker.

An enormous container ship with an orange hull passed by the Ile de Cézembre.

It had rained. The air wasn't entirely clear. It was thick and whitish. It was very cool. Everything glowed brightly.

The mist gradually rose up Simon's back, as he held the handle of his motorboat, and became mingled with the sunshine.

CHAPTER 4

26 August 2010, the empty boat on the sea.

Claire nowhere to be found.

Sunday 29 August 2010, the body, partly eaten by fish, washed up in a pool on the beach.

*

Sunday 29 August 2010.

'I opened the door,' says Paul. 'The two gendarmes knew me. They fixed me with a sad look in their eyes.'

'Claire?'

They shook their heads.

'No, it's the mayor of La Clarté.'

'Simon?'

'Yes.'

'Monsieur Quelen's body has been fished out of the sea at the La Goule cave.'

*

Paul and Jean found Claire sitting in the rain just by the slate plaque to the Lumière brothers. They helped her to stand. Paul forced her to walk to the house. He dragged her by the hand. She was dripping wet.

'Simon's killed himself.'

She was shivering. He dragged her to the bathroom. Jean left them (it was Sunday and he still had two services to conduct, in two parishes, down the coast). Paul ran a bath. He pulled off her pullover. Even her bra was soaking. He took it off. He pulled at her track-suit bottoms. The trousers and pants, gorged with water, came away together. He was surprised to find her body hairless. So long and white. She was beautiful in a way you couldn't have imagined from seeing her walking on the heath all day: a quite simple beauty, gleaming wet, naked and white.

He went to get a towel from the bathroom. He wiped her face, her little gleaming breasts, her ribs, her pale, hollow belly. He couldn't but find her very beautiful. He folded back the sheet, pulled up the blanket, tucked the bedclothes in and switched out the light on the bedside table, while leaving the bedroom door open and the light on in the corridor. He went up to the little sitting room/office/bedroom he had built for himself under the eaves. He took his headphones and put on a record.

*

Efforts were made to claim that it was an accident. Simon had been caught by a tidal current. The lugger was antiquated. It had broken up, capsized inexplicably. It was because of this current that the body had been so quickly carried back to the coast at l'Anse-au-Genêt, etc. (in reality, he had been in the motor boat).

*

'Later, much later,' said Paul, 'it was well after dinner—when she hadn't eaten anything—it was in the evening, I could see her eyes were full of tears and she was making an effort to hold them back. I talked about this, that and the other to avoid her speaking, but she was looking over with her chin jutting out. I could feel the emotion rising in her. I didn't know what to do to prevent it overflowing and getting to me. I hate intimate talk, I hate feelings being expressed. Her lips, which had grown thin and pale, quivered with pain. Her eyes were extraordinarily open and there was a touch of madness in them: 'I saw it all,' she mumbled and she pressed herself against me and, at last, cried until she could cry no more:

'He let himself slip into the water.'

"You dreamt it."

"He gave me a little wave."

I could feel her tears streaming down my neck. I didn't believe her. I just kept on and on stroking my sister's old back.'

PART FIVE

Voices on the Heath

CHAPTER 1

Jean

I loved Paul but I didn't feel any jealousy towards Claire. Claire's world was so far removed from Paul's. I loved Paul and I admired the couple that the brother and sister made. I marvelled at the solidity of the bond between them. Nothing either of them might do was capable of weakening the affection they felt for each other. Neither the brother nor the sister was concerned to examine anything that might have befallen them in the course of their occupations, marriages, resignations or divorces. And, above all, in no circumstances would they have judged anything. The sentiment that prevailed between the two wasn't love. Nor was it a kind of automatic forgiveness. It was a mysterious solidarity. It was a bond without origin, insofar as no pretext or event had at any point decided that that was how it would be. They had, of course, shared some cruel scenes and bereavements as children. They had wept alongside each other. But they had never premeditated or concluded a pact between the two of them. We might even say that, in the early years of their adult lives, they had become more or less indifferent to one another, and perhaps even a little hostile because of the different choices they had made with regard to their childhoods. Yet a complicity had emerged over the years. It had intensified. We might even say a loyalty had imposed itself on them which, as time went on, quite particularly overrode any complications of pride, suspended all criticism and never allowed the slightest irritation to be felt between them.

They could accept anything from each other, even things they didn't understand.

They showed no interest in looking for motives. It was enough for them just to lend each other support. They even accepted the other's whims more readily than their own.

*

In the churches, at every service, I look up before beginning and gaze on people whom I never see out shopping either at the market or on the harbour.

It is always a mystery.

People you don't see anywhere gather in the churches.

In the chapel of Our Lady at La Clarté, there is a fine Madonna with 'visible child'. You have to know Breton for this: visible means naked.

Sometimes, when brothers and sisters don't hate each other, they love each other better than lovers. They are certainly more constant and steady than if they were driven by desire. Furthermore, they have so many more memories behind them than lovers can. The brother or sister knows the other's oldest, most childish, clumsiest, most ridiculous, earliest, coarsest past. They were there when the greatest passions were expressed—the first ones, for the most painful wounds are the ones you can't foresee because you don't know they exist; the ones against which you have no defence; the most unrecognizable; those that well up at the frontier of the origin.

*

One summer's day in 2009, Paul bought an old decorated ridge slate in a bric-a-brac sale I'd organized outside the church at Saint-Briac. He gave it to Claire as a birthday present on 26 August.

'Here,' he said, handing her the parcel. 'I've found you an allegory of truth.'

She took it. She unwrapped the newspaper around it and took a long look.

'Paul, it isn't an allegory of truth.'

She stroked the old slate.

'It's marvellous,' she said. 'I'm really grateful, but it's not Truth.'

'So who's the woman coming out of the well, then?'

'It isn't a well, it's a grave.' (She pointed to the line carved below the jagged upper edge of the slate.) 'It's a Day of Judgement. It's a woman risen from the dead and lifting the stone of her tomb.'

'I didn't mean . . .' said Paul, 'I hadn't thought . . .'

'But, no, it's wonderful, Paul. It's brilliant. I'm coming back to life.'

*

She would eat beechnuts, thin, white, fresh, raw, astringent, delicious beneath their little mitre-shaped husks.

She loved them more than anything—more even than black-clawed crab, though she loved that beyond all measure, calling it by the local name *houvet*.

As she grew older, Claire had taken to gathering the fruits of trees. She piled them on sheets of newspaper on the cooker (Paul no longer used it, he had moved on to Japanese cuisine). All along the cast-iron range, you could see the red berries of the holly (it should be said that, in Breton, *quelen* means holly);

the spiny, half-open, shrivelled burs of chestnuts;

the whirlybirds of the sycamore tree;

the reddish catkins of the ash;

the woody shell of the walnut and its oily, ivory-coloured nut;

the spinning-tops of the medlars;

cobnuts from the hazel tree, wrapped in their pale green hoods.

the acorns from the oak trees, with a hint of crimson and their brown acorn cups.

the black cones of the two cypress trees that had been planted in the new graveyard at Le Décollé.

the blue, downy cones of the juniper tree, all covered in 'bloom'.

This was her personal diary. These were her paths.

*

Paul had barely known his father. He had no memory of him. This pained him and he didn't talk about it much, but he did talk to me about it quite often. The Methuens were from Saint-Cast-le-Guildo. They were descendants of John Methuen. Paul's great-grandparents had known the Lumière brothers when they stayed there in the summer. They rented out one of the villas they had built to them. It was in the cave of la Goule aux Fées below La Clarté in summer 1877 that Louis and Auguste Lumière had made the world's first colour photographs. My friend took me over the clifftops above Saint-Énogat and down into the la Goule cave.

And it was near there, not in the sea but in a pool, at low tide, that the body of the mayor of the port of La Clarté was found washed up in the summer of 2010, partly eaten by crabs, partly mangled by rocks and partly nibbled by fish.

In Breton legend, ghouls or fairies are said to have been unhappy women. The fairies are the rocks that weep in the waves for the dead, whose bodies they break and tear apart. As soon as a rock weeps in its wave, the human being with the good fortune still to be of this world must halt on his seaside path. He must turn his gaze attentively on the crying rock, hail it and ask it its name. That will gradually quiet its cries or, rather, soothe its pain.

Then the noise of the breakers will be quieter.

This is the spirit of Pentecost.

By asking the howling its name, the suffering would seem to go out of the cry and be soothed.

'It is almost prayer,' says Paul.

'Yes, it's even—exactly—what was called an "orison".'

'Might as well say "fairy", then. I prefer fairy,' says Paul.

But I'm no longer listening to the ritual ribbing from Paul.

Suddenly, it strikes me that, when they see Paul's sister with her white hair blowing in the wind, the tourists must sometimes wonder who this old woman is who speaks to the waves and is, apparently, answered by them.

*

I think Paul Methuen's older sister liked to experience the sense of that very ancient time one can read in rocks, the time that burst into life with the sun, the time preceding life, the time driving the sea's waves, the time Jesus constantly speaks of, the time of Advent, the time that is coming but never arrives, the time that goes astray in the astral wind that drives it, the time forever being lost, in a loss that flows away long before its counting begins, long before the calculation of its speed, long before the accumulation of its traces—a horizonless perspective plunging into infinity, an ecstasy endlessly volleying its strange dust into the sky.

God is so old.

God is so old in the tiniest patch of lichen, in the fingernail that lifts it, in the round eye that approaches it—an eye that is the product of the sun.

*

God is older and older.

He rises in a sort of porous mist, more commonly seen at the dawning of the day.

He is scooped out in the sudden hollows which, for millennia, the waves have fashioned in the surface of the sea.

It is true that the liquid mass of the ocean and its damp vapour are so much more archaic than the fur on animals or the bark on trees.

And, even more so, than the tongues of men.

Where Claire was concerned, I thought it was all about kneeling among the rocks, meditating among the rocks, living alongside the beloved past so as to bring it back, to rekindle it, as though with a flame.

She was that blond, white flame mingled with the bush she crouched by.

She made the past burn within itself, as the stars do, which are themselves, quite simply, the past burning.

The aim, in the depths of the soul, was to re-immerse all that happened into the more ancient combustion which, from the very depths of space, continued to advance.

*

The hills are girded with joy, says God.

And the brother and the sister moved forward between the gorse, the hawthorn and the brambles.

It was, every morning, the great morning of a day never seen before.

The over-excited birds sang all over the heath, in the thickets, in the oat fields, in the broom, in the leaves of the trees, amid the bamboo canes; they were drunk with joy, with light, with fresh air, with sunshine.

*

The sky was cloudless, deep and blue.

Above La Clarté, by the Stones, it seemed truly infinite.

*

It made no difference that Claire knew dozens of languages, she just spoke in general of flowers. Flowers of the coast road. Or flowers of the black rocks. Paul, good scholar that he was, used the scientific names, the Latin and English names. I did as he did, though I wasn't myself so scholarly. Claire's daughter Juliette knew how to name everything authentically and how to translate everything back into the common names available to everyone. She spoke of grape-hyacinths, jasiones, catchflies. Among the grey rocks, she spoke of yellow stonecrops. She spoke of blackthorn, borage, dog rose and privet. She showed me everything and taught me everything. She spoke of red fescue, gorse, orache. I liked long, tall Juliette, the teacher of natural sciences. I found endless pleasure listening to her speaking of these things and naming the plants so simply and surely. God is truly the Word. Everything without exception, even the very lowest of things, has an augmented existence once it has been named—a more marked independence, a sumptuousness.

*

The last memory I have of Claire Methuen? She is walking with her arms out to balance herself along the concrete edge of the lobster breeding pond.

She walked endlessly, but walking didn't keep the pain 'at bay'. Walking didn't wipe away the grief over Simon. Walking brings no consolation. Walking makes you think. Each step brings a new thought. Each knee that rises, that pushes on one's cassock, that cleaves the air, brings a question that opens up in turn within one's head. Walking opens up something in a place, bores into something in time. She spoke softly amid the gorse bushes. Paul's sister was thought slightly mad. In reality, she was meditating. I think the elder sister of the man I loved was trying to understand something quite beyond her brother's reach. I think she was discovering a face of which he and I both knew nothing. Of course I don't want to say that Claire Methuen believed, as I do, in God. Perhaps she would have preferred to say she was staring down what was crushing her. Perhaps that is what we can call existing. Then she stopped staring down what was crushing her. Little by little, she began to contemplate what was crushing her.

*

Watching her, it would seem to me that, contrary to the way men are—or at least the way homosexuals are, among whom I must count Paul, myself, and God himself (at least half of Him, since he loves us all and made us all)—women don't desire men the way men desire each other.

Women don't really appreciate the improbable beauty of their manhood.

And women don't seduce men to get their hands on their power or to exert that power surreptitiously or to tame it, or to take their money or to get what they lust after.

Women don't even want children from the men they embrace in order to reproduce them, or to reproduce themselves, or with the aim of sating their urge for vengeance by sending their little ones out to conquer the world.

Women aren't even looking to men for houses in which to grow old and bored beside them.

Women need men to console them for something inexplicable.

*

It's only now, after living so many long years with Paul alongside Claire, that I can see that the path she was following was much more an otherworldly one than the path of her love.

Bushes, cliffs, inlets, caves, islands, boats—these were, of course, always sites that had something to do with Simon Quelen, but Simon's presence was no longer necessary to them.

The marks of her attachment, beautiful as they were, also traced out a kind of route in physical space.

*

One day I had the courage to talk to Claire Methuen one on one: 'Fabienne tells me that you and Paul had a younger sister.'

'That's right.'

'She said she died in the car accident that killed your parents.'

'That's more or less it.'

'But Fabienne told me it wasn't an accident.'

'That's right too.'

'So what was it?'

Claire didn't reply immediately. She got up and went to the window.

'Our mother had decided to leave. Dad didn't want that and he drove the car into the parapet of the cliff road, but the concrete barrier didn't give. Dad and Lena died at the scene. Paul and I survived. Mum too, to tell the truth, but then she committed suicide. But, Jean, don't tell Paul any of this. Or do tell him, I don't mind. But Paul doesn't know. Or doesn't want to know. I don't think he's ever wanted to know.

*

Claire's God was a very violent one. It was the weather. She didn't hide the fact. When everything went dark, when all the elements were suddenly at odds and everything began to roar and thunder and howl, she would say to me, 'Come with me. I love the spectacle of violent rain, storms and tempests. Take Paul's wax jacket. Come on, Jean. Paul has always been "a scaredy cat".'

*

The three big recumbent stones running from the chapel to the headland above the sea weren't Christian. They were much older than the Christian world. But on one of those stones the instruments of Jesus' Passion had been carved. On another, there was an axe surrounded by either snakes or waves.

*

At the end of the day, the horizon grows red.

She would sit outside.

She would pull a chair from inside the chapel and place it outside.

I'd had a key made for her for the chapel of Notre-Dame de La Clarté on the pretext of her seeing to its upkeep and decorating it with flowers. I saw her one day as I was coming up the interminable La Clarté steps after having said Mass in the little low church by the harbour. She was drowsing. She had put a tartan blanket on her lap. I didn't disturb her, but watched from a distance, without making a sound. Paul, Old Man Calève, Juliette or the post lady often watched her, as I did, without disturbing her or sitting down next to her, as she scanned the sea and the horizon, the mysterious boundary line where sea and sky at times seem to touch and merge.

I looked where she was looking, but that day it wasn't the horizon she was watching but the big blue rock that jutted out of the water, that stood out of the grey waves, that stuck out its sparse little pink and brown spikes on the surface of the water.

There were few waves.

The sky was yellowish all over.

The weather was mild.

I was looking at her old sunburned, salt-scorched hands, clasping each other on the blanket.

*

She became really Breton. She planted hydrangeas everywhere, all down one side of the farmhouse, and down the other side too, and on the sandy paths when the holes were too deep, in order to soak up the moisture, the run-off from the gutters when it rained, the water from the rivulets that lay stagnant near the blue granite posts and formed little puddles.

*

In the evening, she would still be walking beside the sea, before she came back to us. The sun was gently slipping into the dark water. She would still linger outdoors. She zigzagged among the shells on the wet sand, alongside the little rolls of the tiniest waves. Suddenly, she told us, one day she heard singing.

She stopped.

It wasn't a melody coming from the sea. It wasn't God speaking to her from up in the heavens. The voice was a woman's. 'A young woman, a very young woman', she said, turning to Paul. 'And it came from the land.'

She walked resolutely, slowly, carefully towards the voice, whose origins were unclear against the noise of the waves as they broke. She crossed the whole stretch of sand and rock that ran towards the West. She climbed the last grey granite rocks. She discovered a gap in the highest of them. It was really a gap in the pink lichen. It took two goes to get her body through the sandstone wall. She slipped in. She tried to edge her way along. Long and thin as she was, she had to wriggle, but eventually she managed it.

She came out immediately on a winding path that ran up the east slope of the cliff.

The path was narrow, grassy and blocked by bushes. She put the straps back on her espadrilles so that she could make headway through the straw, stubble and little stones. There were lots of thistles and she was careful to avoid them. She was wearing a little grey cotton skirt that gave her bare legs no protection from scratches—and, particularly, from the stinging hairs of the big nettle leaves. As evening descended in the west, she walked in the direction the singing was coming from, moving towards the beautiful, golden light. She lifted a glistening gate. She had to make a strenuous effort to heave the bottom of the gate over the oats growing in its way. She had to make an even greater effort, after passing through, to drop it back into its dry mud hole. She put the iron ring back over the post. She viewed the mingled grasses and gorse, the outcrops of clay, the pond and the garden in front of her. She went on and on towards the cliff house. A long lawn pitted with sandy holes ran up towards her. The French windows were wide open. That was where the singing was coming from. The music was getting louder and louder. At the same time as it increased in intensity, it seemed to her to grow more beautiful. A man, visible in profile, was at the cello, facing a woman who almost had her back to Claire and was singing. Another, older—very elderly—woman was at the piano. The musicians saw her through the French windows as she was coming across the lawn. They carried on playing. She smiled and entered. The man playing the cello nodded towards the sofa. She sat down on the sofa. She closed her eyes.

CHAPTER 2
Juliette

My mother was tall and very thin with a domed forehead, hollow cheeks and small, dark, darting, anxious eyes. She had a beauty all her own. At any rate, she walked magnificently.

She had a magnificent bearing, a wonderful gait.

When she was angry, she didn't raise her voice but her face went pale, almost pale blue. It made you fear for her life, so gleamingly translucent did she look, resembling a dangerous heart case. You did as she said.

The black cormorants had become almost tame in her presence. I don't know how she'd managed that. With their little grey crests, they came to say hello.

Mum forever felt the urge to be out of doors. Since the fire which, years earlier, had destroyed the main body of the farm where she lived, any closed space sent her into a panic. A door had only to be locked to plunge her into a sort of apnoea. Any place, even a light and airy one, in which at least one window wasn't left wide open, seemed to her to spell immediate confinement. She hated other people's houses, restaurants in winter, cinemas all year round, the treatment rooms of the thalassotherapy centre and indoor swimming pools.

Everywhere prison, everywhere impatience, everywhere anxiety.

*

She couldn't get into a 403 or a Volkswagen.

*

I remember my Uncle Paul down on his knees outside the newsagent's. He's staring at the brand-new blue padlock he has in his hand, the padlock on the wheel of his bicycle.

I go up to him and ask him what's going on.

'I've forgotten the combination,' my uncle replies.

He looks distraught.

'Try the date of Mum's birthday.'

The padlock opens.

*

They didn't talk much. (When the priest wasn't there, my uncle and my mother didn't talk much.) They often stayed outside after night had fallen, side by side on the garden chairs. They didn't do much. They looked out to sea or up at the clouds. They held hands. When one fell asleep, the other woke them, pulled them by the hand and they went off together to go to bed.

*

When the priest was there, we had to remember to have *Craquelins de Saint-Malo* in. Paul would shout to me: 'Don't forget the Loc Maria crêpes for Jean!'

I remember Uncle Paul preparing a buckwheat pancake: the cloth for greasing the pancake pan, the spreader for the batter, the spatula for lifting out the pancake. It was a living advert for French regional TV.

Mum hated doing the washing up. She hated doing the shopping. She hated going into a supermarket. Uncle Paul did everything. He was also in charge of doing the washing and hanging it out. I remember that he was happy to do it, but he didn't iron. He just hung everything up when it came out of the washing machine. All Claire's clothes, the priest's and mine ended up without too many creases in them, a little rough, slack and strangely porous. Claire, for her part, went wandering. When the priest was there, Paul liked to set about making dishes that took hours to prepare and cook. The three of them were so thin and wandered around the heath and among the rocks so much that they immediately walked off what Uncle Paul cooked in the evening. It has to be said that they only really ate—at least my mother and uncle only ate—in the evening.

*

It should be explained that beyond the beach at Saint-Énogat, beyond the thalassotherapy centre, beyond the headland and cave of la Goule, there was a little town running down to the sea and, right at the bottom, a strange little harbour, that could take just a few trawlers, a few small boats and the launches that ran a shuttle service between the islands and the harbours. The heathland on top of the cliff was exposed. The great recumbent stones—the Pierres Couchées—and the chapel of Notre-Dame de la Clarté, which had more or less Christianized them, had given its name to the little town. Mum, as she grew old, was increasingly concerned with the state of the heath. It's my understanding that Simon Quelen, whom Mum had once loved, and who'd had several terms as mayor of the little port of La Clarté, had also done a great deal, ecologically, to protect the town.

*

The priest went away for a while. His name was Jean. Paul was very unhappy at that time. (The priest had moved in with a conservator at the Saint-Denis museum of art and history.) He came back later.

*

Mum wasn't a smart dresser. You'd see her pitch up in her two-piece swimming costume wearing big shoes that would be sucked down by the sand and the silt. Her bag would bang against her gaunt rear. She'd hold her spiked stick out in front of her, seeking out crabs, including the velvet swimming crab, as she padded between the rocks.

One day, Mum pointed up slowly, gently to the sky and showed me something.

Two birds of prey suddenly came together, came to a stop and then began to spiral downwards vertiginously but face to face, with their wings outstretched and gripping each other by the talons. Ten feet from the waves, they suddenly parted and flew off each in its own direction.

Suddenly, unexpectedly, they came together again and hurtled back up to the top of the cliff where they hid themselves from view. Seldom have I seen anything more disturbing or more beautiful.

*

French ornithologists call a bird that chooses the same spot to spend the winter each year a *revenant*. Herring gulls, black-headed gulls, herons, cormorants are all 'revenants'. Old Man Calève knew all the nests of these returners. He showed me each of these hiding places, one by one, and I thought I'd be able to show them to Mum in turn, but she knew them all. She pointed out other nests that Old Man Calève had missed, for she herself missed nothing.

*

The second time I saw her, when I moved into the farm for a month in summer after Léon left the first time, then, to give me something to do, she showed me round the whole of the place where she lived.

She showed me everything.

'Just look at that,' she'd say.

With Mum, it was always about looking.

'Look at that, it's beautiful.'

She also showed me round the little town.

She greatly admired the town of Saint-Énogat, where she was born, and the little port of La Clarté, where Simon had been mayor.

She showed me the docks, the lock, the two harbour walls, the landing stage where the boats came in just by the café and the post office.

The chandlers and the newsagent-cum-tobacconist's on the ground floor of the building on the corner.

The Grand Stairway.

On the other side, the post office, the harbour café, the baker's the shoe shop.

The shop selling swimming costumes, the estate agent's, the hairdresser's beside the Crédit agricole.

The National Stairway, for that was the insipid—or indigestible—name of the stairway that led up to the town hall.

The telephone box, the municipal noticeboard, the urinal—these were all concentrated on a little terrace one metre square.

That was where her lover had reigned.

She was very fond of the harbour. She liked its grey and black walls. She liked the colour of the sky, much more often white than blue. She liked the dizzying stairways that ran down from the clifftop, stairways cut into the rock from time immemorial, from the time, perhaps, of the recumbent stones themselves. Only the iron handrails dated from the days of the Third Republic. More or less in the middle, on the side of the cliff, when you really got to La Clarté properly so-called, when you arrived at the first slate roofs, when you got to the first houses of the village, there were lighter wooden stairways with aluminium handrails running along the little walls of granite and quartz, making it possible to walk from house to house and terrace to terrace without falling—particularly as, most often, the roofs of the lower houses served as terraces for the ones above.

*

At the end, Mum had completely given up on the little garden at the Ladon farm. She had stopped tending it and begun to manage the entire heath. Admittedly, Uncle Paul had had no answer to the bamboo. He had lost the battle and the bamboo had grown wherever it could around the farm. In the middle of this great bamboo plantation, the lawn became a sort of sad yard. There was no water in the pond now. In summer, it was a kind of peeling yellow moss. Then the moss turned to dust. The rose bushes kept on flowering, but they had grown strange. They were very long, leafless, angular, crooked. All the leaves had been gobbled up by snails. There were snails everywhere. The watering can was full of snails. Dozens of snails huddled together behind the shutters, as though the end of the world were at hand.

In the end, I believe Mum was happy for me to come.

I believe that, at the end of her life, she felt some affection for me. I'd sometimes get a cheery welcome when she saw me at the wheel of my car.

*

Their hair was going white. Even the brown duffle coats uncle Paul and Mum wore had turned grey and white. They both wore shiny tunics full of crystals.

She went out all the time and yet she wasn't suntanned.

Her face hadn't grown brown (as she got older it didn't get brown much any more), but it had become brighter. Her eyes had grown more feverish. Her cheeks were sunken. The attention she paid to everything around her, to all the events that happened, had never been more tireless.

As she grew older, her gaze grew darker and more concentrated.

Her eyes were darkly happy—two little round eyes black as anthracite surrounded by hair that was more white than blond or yellow, ravaged by the salt air.

*

In 2016, Léon had left me for good. I didn't see my sister any more, having fallen out with her over Léon, whose side she took. I couldn't go on, I was tired. I came and spent the whole summer at Mum's. It was hot. The leaves of the trees were covered in dust and riddled with mysterious little holes. The earth was cracked and grey. The grass was yellow, when not completely scorched. I was totally helpless. I'd phoned her (I'd phoned Uncle Paul who passed me over to Mum). She was coming up from the beach when I arrived, driving along the path in first gear. She came towards the car as soon as she saw me, her eyes straining, happy I swear. She looked happy, but she was so thin and her hair was quite dirty—more grey than white. She didn't smell good.

That day she was wearing a none-too-white shirt with none-too-beige leggings. She was barefoot. She showed me something, but she was talking too softly for me to understand. She had very thin little wrists with protuberant little round wrist bones. I look where Mum is looking. I try to see what she is pointing at. She explains: 'The ospreys are remaking last year's nests.'

*

That isn't my last my memory of her. But it was just then, in the July. She was sitting on the bank, her—white—face on the same level as the big white corymbs of the elderflowers.

*

The sea in the distance is still murky, while little islands of light form here and there, white surfaces gradually gilded at the edges: suddenly, there's a green line and something like a muffled explosion that pales in the sky; all of a sudden, her legs go weak at the beauty of it; she sits down on a grey granite rock and now the sun rises.

*

When Claire went up to them slowly, the hawks wouldn't even fluff their feathers or spread their wings.

*

One day, my old mother came and crouched down by me in what remained of the 'garden' amid the bamboo.

It was very hot. I'd pulled up one of the chairs and pushed it out of the door to slip into the shade of the wildly proliferating bamboo in the—wholly relative—cool of the almost empty pond. I'd put a chair in front of me and, with my feet up on it, I was taking a little nap. Speaking softly, Mum said: 'He let himself sink.'

'Are you sure?'

'Yes.'

*

It seems to me that even death didn't separate them. Perhaps even the opposite was true. His death didn't unite them either, but he's there. He's constantly there. He's there with her the whole time. And, conversely, she's with him the whole time. She attends to him. He has become the bay.

Each day she would go and sit in his shadow, in the shadow of the bay; each day she would go and settle into her rocky nook, hide herself just opposite the nest of the great black-backed gull.

My last memory of her? There was a little stretch of grass cut short beside the wall of the farmhouse. That wall, on the other side of the invasive bamboo, was always in the shade. That side of the farm smelt good. It was topped by a big wisteria planted by Uncle Paul, which increased that shade after the end of May. Everything smelt good. It was a hot June day. The two of us sat down beneath the wisteria blossom. In the distance, the sparrows shook their feathers before coming to drink from a cup of water Uncle Paul had left on the ground. All was quiet. It was the two of us there and no one else. No Paul, no Jean, no Simon. Mum took my hand and said not a word. She was breathing lightly. She was breathing a little noisily. As she aged, she had begun to give off a light smell of sweat, hay, salt and sea air; of sea, granite and lichen.

CHAPTER 3

Paul

I first have to explain something that went on inside me which wasn't really of my doing. Something that transformed my personal life from top to bottom. When my sister disappeared, after the farmhouse fire that Simon Quelen's wife started in 2008, when a worried Fabienne Les Beaussais called me in Paris and asked me to come as quickly as possible—or, more precisely, when Fabienne and I didn't find Claire at Mme Ladon's home, as I'd hoped or as Fabienne had led me to believe, when we wandered around Dinard, around Saint-Énogat, when we had to wait at the barrage, cross the Rance, go to Saint-Malo and find the hospital—I believed for some hours that Claire was dead. Life—the life I'd been leading for twenty-five years—broke off there and then. Our existence—the existence of the two of us, which was made up of two parts—broke into two parts within me. Discovering these two discontinuous, detached pieces, I discovered how intimately attached I was to her. Without her eyes on me, I'd no longer be able to live. I was lost without that sure and certain community that the two of us formed. Her sudden disappearance left me feeling empty. It was as simple as that. I discovered I was more lost than she could be. My passion for money was snuffed out at a stroke. Admittedly, this did coincide with the recession. Business suddenly collapsed. But it wasn't just the financial crisis that led me to give up on my activities in Paris, nor that prompted me to sell the flat in the rue des Arènes, since cinema and restaurants, bars, parties and discotheques, friends and friends' bodies also lost their attraction for me.

We found her alive, frozen, sleeping on a tyre.

The oddest of my sister's habits became something seminal.

She preferred muddy paths to big city streets.

Rather than watch television, she'd prefer to sit silently in the mist by a pond or look out to sea and watch motor boats and sardine luggers floating down below the cliffs.

She'd come, in the end, to prefer seagulls and sparrows to chemists and tourists.

Her madness was less serious now, her anxiety attacks having almost disappeared, or, at least, doing so over time.

Her dark, staring gaze stayed with her. She seemed to smile at thoughts that occurred to her, at inner scenes, remembered landscapes, enchanting dreams.

Kneeling among the rocks, her head leaning forward. A white T-shirt, grey leggings. I saw her greyish bottom rise. I went nearer. Her lips were touching the water. She was lapping up seawater, stabbing her tongue into the sea. That same day, when I found her in the kitchen for lunch, I said:

'I saw you just now. You shouldn't drink seawater. It's dirty. And it's extremely salty.'

'Yes, it's salty. I like it. I drink one little mouthful per day.'

'*Per day?*'

'Yes, every day before lunch.'

'Do you realize that water's disgusting?'

'Poor old Paul. If the sea's disgusting, then I don't mind being disgusting.'

*

At the beginning, just after Simon's death, she went there for an hour or two; she was completely prostrate at first, riveted to the spot by pain; then she'd sit motionless at the top of the cliff, just opposite the place where she'd seen him go into the sea.

Because she said she'd seen him climb out of the boat. Here's the scene: the sea opens a little, Simon slips into it, he disappears. That was her version. That was what she told me. I don't think she'd told it to anyone else. Even to Jean. Certainly not to Juliette.

Then it became a full-time occupation. From the moment of sunrise to the last rays of the day, she was there. She was present. She was looking out to sea.

In the morning, before morning, when the sun's rays still hadn't come over the horizon, when it was still night, she left the house.

By the time a milky light crept across behind the outline of the chapel and the rocks, she was already down beside the waves. She was walking along the damp sand, the absolutely fresh sand, the sand that was evermore washed and cleaned, the purer and purer sand that the ocean left behind as it withdrew. She'd follow the delicate, mysterious prints of the birds' tracks in the mud. The water would disappear among the shells, the corpses of crabs, the seaweed, the little hunks of quartz. In the distance, Claire Methuen was looking. Watching.

At nine a.m. she would come back up.

At that same time, the tanker lorry was climbing towards Old Man Calève's farm to fetch the milk.

*

One day she explained to me that after a certain time the landscape would suddenly open up and come towards her and it was the place itself that inserted her into it, that suddenly contained her, protected her, relieved her of her loneliness, cared for her. Her skull emptied into the landscape. Then her bad thoughts had to be hung on the asperities of the rocks, the brambles, the branches of the trees and they stayed there. Once she was completely empty, the place stretched out before her as much as it did within her. The foliage unfolded. The butterflies and flies and bees began to flutter around fearlessly. A field mouse had rushed out and come towards her knees. An owl had landed on a rock covered in yellow lichen and neither of them had felt any fear or threat. It was as though she were no longer a human being, as though for other creatures she no longer represented the danger of a human being or a predator or destroyer. Smells came to her more intensely, all of them recognizable—the scents of the earth, of mint, of hazel trees, bracken and moss.

Gradually the lights went out, the colours dimmed, the silence grew; twilight reached her, the shadows enveloped her and night fell—she became all that at the same time as it was happening.

And she was the night.

Her eyes closed.

One morning, quite a while before she was transferred to Cancale, Fabienne the Dinard postwoman had found her sitting dazed on the coast road. She didn't know who or where she was but she was calm. It wasn't Fabienne but Évelyne from the estate agents who called me.

Fabienne had driven Claire to a little clinic at Dinan, where I caught up with her.

She had the face of a child.

The nurse: 'She woke up at two a.m. shouting for all she was worth. I rushed to her room, guided by the noise. She asked, "Where am I?" I answered that she was in a clinic. She screamed out a name. I have to warn you, Mr Methuen, she's rather confused.'

'What did she shout?'

'Simon.'

Silence.

'Is that your name?'

'No, it's the name of someone we know. We're talking about a friend who lived in a neighbouring village.'

*

After that, I'd go looking for her all over the place when night fell, but I wasn't worried. To me, it had become like taking a walk. Having said that, I'd find her up on the clifftops more and more, in the field with the Recumbent Stones, leaning against the wall of the chapel. That was probably the place she most liked to be when there was too much wind and no tourists. Jean had given her the key. She wasn't at all anxious any more. The feverish excitement had gone. I'd find her happy in the middle of the night, her knees pulled up against her chest, rocking gently back and forth, looking at the sea and listening to it rise in the darkness.

Nothing of what Fabienne, Noëlle or Évelyne said about Claire matched up with what I thought I'd seen in her. But they knew her better than I did. When they were children and teenagers, they had lived alongside her themselves. As for me, from the days when, as a small child, I'd look up admiringly at my sister, an unpredictable fear would suddenly overtake me, something frightening would suddenly loom up from the way she walked, from her silences, and was immediately stifled. It was always something secret, encrypted. As she got older, my sister grew distant from Jean and myself. She had no concern at all for Jean. Naturally, that made me unhappy. But she turned away from everyone else too.

*

Everything I'm saying seems to me to be true, but I've never understood my sister well. I loved her, but she intimidated and overawed me. She was older than I was. She was a girl. She frightened me a little. Often I said to myself, 'Perhaps you haven't fully understood.'

*

I was convinced she possessed some secret I might have got to know more of, if she'd been willing to let me question her.

But from that point on everything was directed towards Simon.

Everything, with her, was directed to the distant figure of Simon on the quayside at La Clarté, to the small white boat he pushed into the sea when he was on the beach at Saint-Énogat, to the lugger whose sail he furled in the marina at Dinard.

Even when lost, he remained her lodestar.

There was a very dull, but very intense dynamic around her body; regularly discernible, it quivered around her, like a circular wave, like an oppressive force.

I could feel this magical circle when I walked for hours beside her; I could feel it, but I couldn't enter it.

*

I didn't believe in God. None of us and no one around us believed. Jean believed in Him for all of us.

*

Some birds make sounds that are barely conceivable. In our garden (the farmhouse garden which, as a result of my negligence, had become a field of Japanese bamboo) and on the heathland above La Clarté, there was a chubby nightingale with a really feeble, quite pathetic song.

But just beyond the first car park at the Pierres Couchées, at the Pointe du Roc, by the shed where the thalassotherapy centre kept their dustbins, there was a magpie that was always trying to find extravagant ways to resolve its songs. It improvised some magnificent, quite incomparable variations. It would sing at 9 a.m. At a quarter to nine, I'd be sitting on the moss by the edge of the sandy path that ran beside the hedge or, if it was wet, I'd be on the pavement where the dustbins were. And I'd be waiting eagerly to hear what it could come up with. One time, a charming elderly client coming out of the Novotel mistook me for a beggar, but he got used to my presence. He'd greet me formally as he passed, as I sat there among the bins. Doubtless he imagined that the man sitting among the dustbins was hungry or after a drink or mad. I'm sure it never entered his head that this was just a man listening to a genius of a bird that sent shivers down his spine with the beauty of its song.

*

Sometimes, coming back from my own walks, I'd find her sleeping in the grass; she was near the farmhouse pond and hadn't moved. One day I stumbled on her naked, a very sad, naked old woman, lying curled in a deck chair in the shade of the dead hazel trees that had been overrun by the bamboo.

*

When I tidied her up after she came back from her wanderings covered in mud, salt, sweat, twigs and little bits of shell, when I saw my sister clean and scrubbed up, I was always surprised to find her so beautiful. She was well-proportioned, though probably a little too thin and much too flat-chested, but increasingly beautiful. Her bottom was small, but twelve hours walking a day had made it firm and muscular. She had no stomach to speak of. She had a tiny sex and her groin area was depilated. I've no idea at all why she was entirely hairless there. I never saw her in the company of other men, apart from Simon. Even her husband I met only on the day of their wedding and I can't recall his face at all. Had she known many men? When had she stopped frequenting them? There was nothing in her room to suggest memories of that order. It was almost empty. Mine was full of records (Jean's office is full of family souvenirs, holy images and works of philosophy). There was very little in hers, very few clothes. Not even language dictionaries. No pictures on the walls. In the big wardrobe, two out of the four shelves were empty. One day, when we were eating, I asked: 'Have you never been in love with other men?'

She regarded me with astonishment. 'Yes, of course.'

'Meaning what?'

'Meaning I was once really in love.'

'Who with?'

'Why, with Simon.'

'But why, in that case, did you split up after the lycée?'

'Simon went to Rennes and I went to Caen.'

'I know all that, but why did it come to an end?'

'Actually, I was the one who broke it off.'

'That's not true, is it?'

'Yes, I stopped answering his letters.'

'Why was that?'

'They were childish, the letters of a kid. I was too much in love to stand for that.'

'And you gave up sex?'

'No, not at the time. But what's that got to do with you?'

She got up.

'Do you have any more silly questions?'

*

Claire said to me: 'I have to tell you a little story that'll be painful for you, but you're nearly sixty. You're big enough now. You're big enough, perhaps, to know the truth. It'll soon be fifty-five years since this happened. That'll be fifty-five years that you've had your eyes and ears closed. We were still living at Saint-Énogat. It had been raining for days and days. It was late afternoon and I was coming back from choir. The curé had insisted on bringing us back in his 2CV. You see, we're really Breton: there are only priests in our lives. When we got to the house, I took my satchel, opened the car door, shouted, "Goodbye, Monsieur le Curé," summoned all my strength and dashed out in the pouring rain. It really was horrendous weather. I ran to the door. I already had my key in my hand. I opened the house door as quickly as I could. I was soaked to the skin. I tore my clothes off and dashed to the bathroom to dry myself. I can still see myself pushing the door open. Mum's stretched out there in the bathtub. The water's red. She's slashed her wrists.'

'Mum died in the car accident.'

'No.'

'Mum didn't die in the accident?'

'No, Mum killed herself two days after the accident in which you were injured.'

'Was she driving?'

'No, Dad was.'

'The accident,' adds Claire, 'in which our sister died.'

'Our sister?'

'Yes, Lena.'

'Marie-Hélène?'

'If you prefer.'

I sank to my haunches. I was incredibly shocked. I said: 'I didn't know I had another sister.'

'You're lying. The proof is that you know her real name.'

'I'm not lying.'

'You've just said her real name.'

'I swear, I didn't know I had a sister other than you.'

To mark my sixtieth birthday, crying seemed the right thing to do.

'No need for tears. You hated her. She was just a year younger than you.'

'Where was I?'

'You were in hospital.'

'Why didn't I know anything about this?'

'At first you thought everyone had died in the accident. You even thought I was dead. They weren't going to tell you all the details.'

'Why not?'

'I don't know.'

'Why wasn't I told more?'

'They just told you I was alive, since you thought I was dead, and that's all!'

'Why don't I remember that sister?'

'Because you don't want to.'

'How old was she?'

'Three. In fact, you're right, she was called Marie-Hélène. But we called her Lena because Mum had decided it would be that way.'

'That's just your stories.'

*

Claire used to make some exasperating remarks. About cooking, for example. Claire didn't cook, had never been able to cook, but passed endless, quite unfairly severe comments on anything original I came up with.

'Auntie 'Guite didn't cook chicory the way you do.'

'You really get on my nerves, Claire.'

When she wasn't in very good shape, she would talk to Aunt Marguerite like an imaginary friend:

'Our aunt wouldn't have liked your recipe.'

'Leave me alone.'

'Auntie 'Guite put sugar in the chicory to counteract the bitterness.'

'Stop it, Claire. Get out a bit. Go down to the sea. Go look at your sweetheart's boat and let me make dinner.'

*

On the heath, near the shell of the old Citroen lorry, there was a very tall but rather ragged beech tree. Though its upper branches reached up into the sky, it was clearly teetering and living out its last days. But, most importantly, there were two highly gifted blackbirds that frolicked in the moss and hay at the foot of the tree. They weren't there at dawn but came at around seven or eight. First they played. Then they jumped into the branches and competed. 'Competed' is putting it mildly: at times, they really let rip. In that case, they could improvise on four styles, carrying on each other's efforts—challenging each other—always on a four-part basis. It was incomparably beautiful.

*

Claire too was a 'virtuoso'. She'd even become a complete 'expert' in meteorology. She knew the hours, all the moments within each tide and each hour. She knew just what time it was by the light. Some musicians have prefect pitch. She had a perfect sense of time. She was directly connected to the sun. She was no doubt drawn to beauty, there can be no denying that. But it was rather mysterious, because there were many places which she never stopped at for a moment that seemed much more beautiful to me. Perhaps those stops were dictated by comfort, by something to sit on, by silence or by absorption—I don't know how to put it. Or perhaps other reasons guided her, relating to plants or levels of sunshine or shade, smells and fragrances, the way the wind blew, or her favourite flowers. She took care of these special places. From the granite, the quartz, the seams of black dolerite, the pink sandstone, the lichen, the moss, the sand and the seaweed, she cleared away all the paper bags, corks, bottle tops and other litter, the twigs, gulls' feathers, cigarette butts and dried seaweed, which she stuffed into the dirtiest backpack I've ever seen. She'd stop, take it off, open it up, fill it, tamp down the contents, close it again and put it back on her shoulders. She really was a mad old woman. Suddenly, she'd sit down. She'd look. She'd set off again. She'd get to another cleft in the rocks, another site.

*

With her white hair and black eyes, her face sunken and thin.

'What's going on?'

She'd shrug her shoulders. She'd turn her back on me. She'd slip one leg under the other. She'd pretend to eat. She'd stir her soup with her spoon.

'Nothing.'

'For my sake, please eat. You're too skinny.'

'At school when I was little, out in the playground Simon would say, "You look like a chest X-ray".'

*

I'm not sure Simon understood much about Claire—any more than I did. There was no doubt he loved her. And he was, no doubt, a good pharmacist, with lots of physical courage, a good manner, style, ruggedness and good looks; he was sportsman, lifeboatman, fireman and mayor. But I doubt he ever fully understood the film in which he'd been cast in the leading role.

*

In the old Charpenterie de la Marine boatyard at Saint-Malo one day, Jean and I came face to face with Simon, his wife and their son amid wooden boat frames, keels and the scents of Oregon pine and African pearwood.

For a good quarter of an hour I listened to the priest and the mayor conversing seriously about fishery issues in the European Union.

*

The last time I saw Simon was at La Clarté. He was sitting on a step outside the chemist's shop, he didn't look well and he was smoking. He wasn't allowed to smoke in his dispensary. He was looking at the harbour.

I got off the shuttle boat and went over to him on the quayside. He was sitting staring into the setting sun, his back against the concrete, his elbow on the step above. You could hear the horns of returning boats in the distance, near the lighthouse. I was forced to pass him to get to the steps going up to the chapel.

'Hi, Simon.'

Simon greeted me cursorily, went very red and moved to let me pass.

*

When Simon died, the priest at Saint-Lunaire refused his blessing on the suspicion of suicide. That was wonderful for me. What threads our lives hang by. It was the opportunity of a lifetime, as I immediately took it as a pretext to call Jean, who had left me at that point.

Jean came immediately, that is to say, the very next day, by the one p.m. train.

Our reunion was silent, ardent, solid and definitive on the concrete platform of the TGV station at Saint-Malo.

It was Jean who organized Simon Quelen's funeral (as he had done so well for Mme Ladon). It was a very different service, a thing of deliberate magnificence, at Gwenaëlle's express request. But Jean, perfect as ever, simply said something like this beside the tomb—a bit better than this, no doubt, but very simple:

'God is sad. God himself says that he is sad. "Tristis est anima mea". But God doesn't speak only of his sadness. He says he is so disgusted with life that he has gone so far as to dream of dying. He says his soul is so sad that he wants not to exist at all any more. Then God repeats: "My soul is sorrowful, for I have reached the point where I desire death".'

*

After Simon died, there was peace. A strange, total peace descended on Claire. An unassailable peace came over her. It was like that every day from that point on. Everything was over and she was simply surviving that completion. Or, rather, she was a participant in it. She still wandered around the world in pursuit of her love, watching her love from a distance, as though everything had ended long ago. She went around on the heath, where she saw her walks through to the end. If it rained, she walked slowly beneath a last rain of the day. She no longer protected herself from anything. She would go down to the sea, which can almost be described as eternal when one stares at it long enough and compares its origins to the age of human beings or the invention of cities and houses. Claire had become Simon and become the place. Nothing held any fear for her any more. Everything was sublime. She was at home everywhere; she was like the very beginning in the dawning of things. She was in the strange, effervescent, radical peace of the upsurge of everything, of the point when nothing can be reversed any more—the excitation that erects, the flower that grows, the flight that soars, the cloud that passes, the joy that dilates, the bird's beak that sings. From this point on, she was without the slightest worry, totally confident, like the little children who stretch out their hands and grasp things and almost invent them in their first grasping. She was like the green that gradually bursts through in the buds of the trees in spring. She was like the yellow and the russet on apple skins in autumn. She was like dew at dawn, like the diaphanous quality in the day's air, like the smell of elderflowers that rises from the hands of lovers and which they wipe on the moss.

Even when it came to peeing and shitting, I discovered by chance that she preferred to do these things out in the countryside, by certain rocks or plants.

She would immediately, promptly, cover the traces with dust, moss and leaves.

She belonged to someone else.

She belonged to the place.

*

She did, however, agree to fall in with some of my habits. She agreed to leave the door closed when sleeping. She opened it as soon as dawn began to break, when she slipped out into the first glimmers of light and the birdsong. On the heath she'd follow the singing of the birds as it grew. She'd see the strange milky air as it silently issued from the gaps in the cliffs. The sky was far from lightening yet. The clouds hadn't yet formed. She would walk in the cold towards the intensely black line of as-yet-opaque umbrella pines, with the grey briar patch immediately behind. Then the day, long before the sun arrived, would be born upon the sea. Then the islands, one by one, would be covered with a sort of light vapour. The birds that had slept on beyond their early morning calling, would begin, one by one, to stir themselves, unruffle their feathers, flap their wings in the branches. Each day, the sun would appear in ever-purer, ever-more refined, ever-more unpredictable density, modesty, splendour or weakness. Colours would be reborn at the same time as individual songs. The sea's waves began to whiten and were hollowed with shadow. The thistle heads grew bluer. The crow's feathers turned blacker and shinier. Claire went along first by the umbrella pines, then took the coastal path of the Customs men and fishermen, before suddenly veering off among the coast's most dangerous rocks, its deposits of rusty scrap metal, its less presentable inlets, its broken-down fishery and its dumps for old tyres. Later on—much later—she'd come back between eight and nine covered in dew, freezing, running a little; she'd open the kitchen door again and the shutters, heat some water and make breakfast. It just remained for me to go downstairs.

She'd become jealous. (If Jean had slept over with me, she wouldn't make breakfast.)

*

Most often she'd sleep curled up on the blue sofa downstairs, with her head on her outstretched arm and her fist clenched.

*

Paths that once led somewhere stop at the edges of the fields.

Others fade out mysteriously up on the clifftops among the pebbles.

Others plunge into thickets, where they disappear.

I think my sister was a lost path overlooking the sea.

I'd been happy under an old sunshade beside a curé in a black turtleneck jumper sitting in his recliner and drinking his aperitif by a dense patch of brambles. Then darkness flooded in amid the bamboo. We had to switch on the light on Jean's harmonium, I had to bury my face in the black turtleneck and its scent of wool.

I'd meet up with him again at the discount religious bookstall at the Diocesan House on the rue de Brest, a stall tended by Évelyne who did his bookkeeping for him.

*

In the cities, where power and money have their home, we never imagine the corners people piss in, the disused wharves, the relics of old dockyards and stables, the run-down alleys, the warehouses, the strange industrial estates and the tiny jungles that sprout up in them, which we're not aware of because we only ever go there by car. In just the same way, we aren't aware of what is hidden from view beyond the sea walls and the luxury villas of the seaside resorts, behind the supermarkets, the fields, the small factories and the garages of the hinterland. And, as soon as there's an area along the coast without a beach, without a restaurant, without access or that isn't overlooked, we can't imagine the degree to which squalor has free rein—with the incomprehensible tipping sites, the improbable treasures, the zones of spontaneous nature and life.

At the cliff edge, there's a tyre, a yellow bush and a piece of dry seaweed.

It is always near to it, near the yellow bush, that she sits and dreams in the evening. Every evening it's the same dream: she dreams she's living with him, she tells him about her day. She relates the events of the day and asks him what he thinks.

*

My last memory of her? It's the memory of the last evening. In fact, of all the evenings when it rained. We're eating in the kitchen. Night fell long ago. It's pouring down outside. She's holding a cigarette or a glass of wine. She takes a swig of wine, which calms her. She gets up. She's standing with her forehead pressed against the windowpane. She wants to go out but it's raining.

CHAPTER 4

Cousin Philippe Methuen

Looking at the wooden 'For Sale' sign, I thought to myself, either Claire's dead or she's put the Ladon farm up for sale and gone off to live in the Maldives. When we were teenagers, my brother and I, we said she was an Arab. We did so because her mother was Muslim. It's true she was Muslim. She was Greek. So we said she was either Turkish or Greek. She was called Depastas. She was wonderful and spoke every imaginable language. Our father's brother, who was an architect and a master mason at Dinard, had got her pregnant. She married our uncle, then decided to leave him. So our father's brother killed himself. Then she killed herself afterwards. She was much more beautiful than Marie-Claire.

'Is it Claire or Chara?'

That's all a sham. Her name's Marie-Claire. No question about it. Our mother forced her on us throughout our teenage years. She was very tall. She always had immensely long legs. And always badly dressed. Big pullovers always, black jeans, rubber boots. We got our own back as best we could. She drove us mad with her good marks. She read the obscurest of languages without even bothering to study them. In summer we let the two cousins know they weren't welcome. But they didn't mind. They were always well aware that we were the real children of the family. So they went off on their own. Off across the fields. They went down through the camp site to the Grève des Marais. She—it was mainly she—began to avoid us. She even began to avoid our father. It was just Paul, the little cry-baby, the little boarder at Pontorson, who followed her about like a shadow. He was a bit of a sissy. She gave him a hard time, bullied him, but however badly she treated him, he followed her everywhere and copied her in everything.

At the farm, as soon as she was in the room, the tension became unbearable.

The fact that our father and mother never agreed on anything was down to her.

I can still remember the smell of the tablets in my mother's bedroom—tablets she took because of her. It was Mother, not our father, who'd wanted to take her in. To tell the truth, I don't know what our father thought about it. I'd have to say that, after his brother's suicide, the series of unfortunate events just went on and on. I remember one day the postman sat down at the farmhouse table. He took the glass of wine my mother had handed him, drank it, put it down on the table and said:

'You have to stop this cycle of misfortune, Marguerite. Go and see the man who has the hardware shop at Tréméreuc. He's from Le Routot.'

'I don't believe in all that stuff,' my mother had replied.

'What possible harm is there?' the postman said. 'And no one's asking you to believe anything.'

Then he got up and left. I can still see him. I'm telling this badly, but it was striking, this warning the postman gave my mother. They must have talked about it in the village before sending him out to Pont Touraude. That must have been going round in our father's head, because the very evening of the day the postman came—or the next evening—he set fire to his armchair as he was smoking his pipe. Around that same time, the tractor began constantly to break down. Then our father got eczema, really bad eczema, to the point where it stopped him sleeping. So he went over to Tréméreuc. It worked very well, the whole lot of us were back on the rails within a few months. After school the girl stayed and worked with the chemist's son. We were more relaxed. Of course, she was the cause of it all. She had much too much force about her. Even her little brother Paul, the boarder at Pontorson, couldn't bear her. He did what she told him, but he couldn't stand her. All he wanted was to get back to boarding school. From noon on Sunday, after Mass, cousin Paul was keen to get back to the school, to his pal and his music. This was the agreement: once she'd been put under their guardianship, the Quelens, the chemist and his wife, would have Marie-Claire at their house on schooldays, after classes, with little Simon who was in the same class as she was. It was a sort of half-board. At the weekend, she was back at our uncle's house (the house of her father, the mason) at Saint-Énogat. And, of course, it was also up to her to look after her young brother on the occasions when he came home from Pontorson.

*

One day our mother found Marie-Claire in tears, in the yard, hunched up near the well, sitting on her school satchel. The little girl was terrified. Our mother asked her who on earth she was afraid of and why she didn't come in. But she held firm and didn't tell on us. She said it was the tawny owl in the oak tree. Then our father came out with his great line: 'In that case, she should go to Le Routot.'

*

I saw her sometimes at Old Man Calève's. We'd embrace, but not warmly. She came to my daughter's wedding. She always liked Mireille because Mireille's like my mother. In the end, she knew everything about the heath, the paths, the shoreline, the nests, the camp sites, the forge, the garage, the dumping grounds for old cars. She knew all about the hideaways where the gangsters sold their drugs, the deals done in the caravans. She knew where the birds of prey, the wasps, the hornets and the snakes nested, and where the smugglers hid their motorboats.

The brother and sister would steal anything they could get their hands on.

She even stole a mother's love.

I know that with Paul, and Simon Quelen too when he became mayor of La Clarté, she did property deals on the sly. And a priest from down the coast was involved too on the quiet, a homosexual of course. She bought up everything, even the fisherman's hut where she and the chemist made love, near the desalination plant.

*

As for Old Man Calève, he just took cigarettes from her, that's all. He wasn't in the habit of smoking. He only smoked when he was sitting at the table with her in the main room at the farm. He had a curious way of smoking. He began by sitting down. He poured her a little glass of wine, poured one for himself, then took the cigarette Marie-Claire had given him between his thumb and his forefinger, squeezing it very tight. He took a little puff and then suddenly stretched his arm a long way from his body, as though he were afraid of the smoke.

She'd drink her wine.

He'd smoke his cigarette.

They wouldn't speak.

*

My last memory of her? At the solicitor's, wanting everything for herself—and getting it.

CHAPTER 5

Noëlle, Andrée, Catherine, Fabienne, Julie, Louise

'It was thanks to Claire that I got a waitressing job at the restaurant in the Dinard thalassotherapy centre,' said Noëlle. 'She'd hardly ever go to the best-known places. The people in the villages took some time to cotton on to her endless wanderings round the countryside. Except for Fabienne, who went all up and down the coast as far as Saint-Énogat, crouched over the handlebars of her post-office bike. But gradually, word got round. The people of Saint-Énogat and Saint-Lunaire came to know this young woman who drank seawater. She was thin and a bit dirty and always had a packet of cigarettes in her hand. She was outdoors all the time. She lived outdoors. Even in high winds. Even in storms. Even in snow showers. Having said that, the residents weren't afraid of her; they didn't feel at all apprehensive, since she was so unobtrusive, timid and quite good looking. Even when she dressed badly, she had something about her. And then they knew who she was. She'd been a child here.'

*

'At the end, when I went to her house,' said Madame Andrée, 'when I did a bit of cleaning there, I never heard her. She'd become really furtive. In trainers, a little skirt or leggings and a cotton T-shirt, thin and light as she was, she'd move as silently as a shadow—the way a shadow creeps over things. She'd come up behind you without you realizing she was there. She'd pass through a door with no more noise than a cloud blotting out the light of the sun. She'd climb stairs without you hearing her body weigh on them.'

*

Catherine (the masseuse from the thalassotherapy centre) claimed Mme Methuen was less mad than they said. Time and again, she'd tell anyone willing to listen that Claire was a crafty one. And that the solicitor had said she was the richest person in the area. She was heir, though no one knew quite how, to an old piano teacher who'd worked in Dinard. She'd bought up the whole headland from Saint-Énogat to La Clarté. At the lower end of the heath, she'd pulled down the little houses, together with the old forge that the thalassotherapy masseuse's father had turned into a garage not so long ago. She'd built some little gentrified villas, summer-cottage style. You can't see any of them from the road. They're hidden by trees, one among hazels, another in beeches, a third in pines, etc. You can't see them. It's a good scheme, ecological, well thought out, just her sort of thing.

*

'It's true I'm a little less close to her than I was. After Mme Ladon died, when I had my two children, I concentrated wholly on them. *She* had thoughts only for Simon, but I respected that. I can even say I always liked her. She was a very straightforward girl, very direct, very all-or-nothing. I went to live at Cancale because of my husband. I managed to get transferred over there. She sometimes came to see me at Cancale, riding in the milk tanker. Don't listen to everything they say about her. You can't be liked by everyone. She could seem stuck-up or indifferent. She wasn't trying to please anyone, because she loved just one man. All her reserve came from that: she loved Simon, she was reserved for just one man. Remember, I watched all this business from primary school onwards. At bottom, she was almost a virgin. One single cause guided her action: the love she felt for Simon. And there's something people missed: the 26th of August was Claire's fiftieth birthday.

The police didn't spot that. Paul understood right away. Just between us, what a strange birthday present! Once, just once, I tried to talk to him about that. But he clammed up like an oyster. I couldn't get him to say a thing.'

*

Julie Treut (the school-bus driver): 'There was a camping table on the pavement, folded up and leaning against the dustbin. The old Methuen woman took hold of the camping table and unfolded it. She put it down gently on the pavement. She looked at it for quite some time. She suddenly folded it up again and carried it off under her arm, but before she'd gone more than a few steps she came back and put it up against the big black plastic dustbin again. That's the last time I saw her.'

*

Madame Andrée didn't think much of the two women painters who'd moved in at Saint-Briac.

'The two women with the beach restaurant at Saint-Briac said spitefully that Mme Methuen "hung about". She didn't hang about. She would carefully retrace the steps she had just taken and that would always, inexplicably, lead her somewhere new. The wind, a different light, the song of a bird, sea spray, a darker or brighter rock, some little yellow flowers—anything could lure her away. She no doubt got lost. But who doesn't get lost? The two women from the restaurant on the beach at Saint-Briac were even "crazier" than she was when they claimed she was "dirty". She washed herself in the sea several times a day.'

'In the pools on the beach.'

'But several times a day.'

*

'This girl, pale-looking in her brown hood,' said Louise, 'was like a beechnut in its cupule. And a sundial into the bargain. She'd established various points in space where she'd stop. She toured around the heath and above the rocks in a manner as regular as the shadows and the passing minutes. In winter, whatever the weather, you'd see her brown hood popping up from one point to another, and you could tell the time by it.'

CHAPTER 6

Old Man Calève

In November, at the end of the month of November, at the beginning of December, when the days are at their shortest, there's no one up on the heathland overlooking the sea any more. Personally, winter and summer, I have to go over the top of the plateau when I'm on my tractor. I'll describe the operation for you: I come round the chapel car park, drive up there to where the wind blows. I brake and slip into first gear, then I make my U-turn, running precisely along the semi-circular path of the Promenade des Pierres Couchées. I catch a glimpse of the sea there and drive on down the path through the gorse, passing the shell of the old Citroen lorry.

In winter, when the leaves are gone from the trees in the wood, you can see the slates on the roof of the main building of the Ladon farm. It was that roof that burned.

I never saw a woman who more liked walking than my neighbour. She could walk for fourteen, fifteen or sixteen hours at a stretch, without stopping. Moreover, she was a young woman who could happily skip meals.

She must have had ankles of steel.

She was always up before I was—even though I get up at five.

While I was struggling to start my own work, I'd see her silhouette flitting about in the rocks as night ended. You'd see her warming herself in the sun in clefts in the granite that must have kept their heat from the day before. Or she'd be sheltering from the wind with her back against the wall of the chapel of Notre-Dame de la Clarté. In the beginning, I imagined her always with a book in her pocket. In my mind, I'd see her sitting on a tree trunk or in a depression in a rock, reading for hours on end, smoking her cigarette, then setting off again quite haphazardly. But I learnt I was completely wrong about that. She didn't read at all. Never in her life did she borrow a book from the public library. I know Mme Restein who runs the lending library, I was engaged to her once. She never saw her. Mme Methuen lived without working and without reading. She roamed around in silence, everywhere, every day that God sent. She was a yellow-and-white-maned woman of the hills. She was even more uncivilized than I am, and that's saying something. She was known as a friend to the caves of the coast.

I really liked her.

I think she went a bit strange in the head. She began to feel pity for everything—for ponds, gulls, bamboo, trees, stones. After cleaning up the whole of the ravine, she cleared up the whole plateau. She weeded. She picked up the dead wood. She gathered up the litter left by tourists and put it in a bin bag. After every shower, she'd tidy up the course of the streams again and sort out the ponds. Sometimes she even sowed seeds.

When Monsieur Quelen's body was found on the foreshore by the Grotte de la Goule, I was the one who called the emergency services.

Later I went to find Mme Methuen on her rock.

'I don't know what to say,' I said to her.

She touched my hand.

The same with Monsieur Methuen in the kitchen at the farm. The gendarmes had just been.

'Where's Claire?' he asked me.

'In her corner. Her place in the bushes,' I told him.

I went out into the yard and showed him where I'd sent the ambulance men to find the mayor's body, so they could get down to the cave. Then he thanked me, turned his back and went off in that direction. He too stopped at the top of the cliff. From a distance, he watched the emergency people down below. He didn't disturb them. He lit a cigarette. He watched the whole thing to the end.

When the two of them walked, the brother and the sister, there was a harmony between them that was amazing to see. Yet he was really small and she was very tall, but it was magical. They sped along, walking quite quickly. They didn't really speak to each other. They'd stop and take a look at something, then go on, all the while pointing things out to each other. They'd drift apart and then wait for the other to catch up, as though bound together with a piece of elastic. Everything was incredibly relaxed and there wasn't the slightest impatience. They were never impatient with each other. I've never seen that in other human beings. Now he's gone off with Father Jean, who was in love with him. But that's another story. That disgusted all the villagers on the coast.

I'm sure I'll remember her, but not her as a person. What I mean is that I don't miss her, not the personality of Mme Methuen and so on. It's her body that's absent from our days. Her body's already missing from the places, the rocks. She's missing from the stairs at La Clarté, which she was the only one to use and which she climbed effortlessly right to the end. She's missing from the little nooks and crannies, from the hiding places where she watched the nests and the burrows, the smaller boats and the luggers on the sea.

*

My last memory of her? A flock of gulls gathering on the sea wall and crying out louder and louder around a scarf—a rather dirty, abandoned scarf lying around on the ground near the bush.

*

In the end, she knew everything about this place better than I do. The little breeze that rustles the leaves of the bushes creates special little round waves on the sea. The wind that stirs the branches of the hazel trees makes for turbulent easterly seas. The clouds that cast their shadows over the fields of maize . . . she could interpret everything better than I could. We talked and she taught me things. When the gulls sheltered in the rocks, she would come and warn me.

*

The postmistress was her friend. She let her deliver the last letters of her round when it was too difficult to pedal against the wind in the sandy or muddy paths up on the heath. It was Mme Methuen who walked across the clifftops to take their letters to the two ends of the village—those who lived near Plage-Blanche and, here, at la Ferme du Roc. She called this farm La Tremblaie, the Aspens. There are people who call it that. That was the name the old Ladons used. They said it was written that way on the title deed. I prefer to call it la Ferme du

Roc. That's what my father called it. When she brought me the mail, I gave her her milk in return. She also got her few provisions from me. She'd choose her eggs by their colour. She'd go and pick her lettuces herself and she'd be the one who'd work out the price. She'd put the little coins on the table and, to be honest, it was never enough.

Sometimes she'd stare at me with her deep black eyes.

I couldn't resist.

She never answered right away. She didn't speak much, but always very politely. She said thank you. When she stood stock-still as a stone on the cliff, that was because she was looking at her sweetheart down below, in his fishing lugger, on the sea.

Can you smell that? It's the smell of the sea. It smells of the sea here all the time. The sea air. There's very little smell of the earth here. For a farmer, it's really strange. None of my fields smells of anything much but the sea. The bushes don't smell of much. The thistles don't smell of much. Or the holly. There's only the brambles, which, for six months of the year, have the smell of blackberries hanging over them.